TBD

-TO BE DETERMINED-

By

Patricia E. Gitt

Second Edition ISBN: 978-1-7341584-6-5
First Edition ISBN: 1519376073

This book was printed in the United States of America

Also by Patricia E. Gitt
CEO
ASAP -as soon as possible –

    A settling of scores

FYI An Unintended Consequence

Book Interior Design by Soumi Goswami |
soumi.goswami.pub@gmail.com

Published by:
Athena Book Publishing
New York, New York
Athenabookpublishing.com

In memory of Ellie Cooper who loved
mysteries in fiction and in life.

"The jealous are troublesome to others,
but a torment to themselves."

— *William Penn*

1

Having arrived at her office at seven o'clock, and before she'd cleared her wine-sodden brain with coffee, Katherine Cunningham was hit with the jarring sound of her phone. It had been Mr. Sweeney's personal assistant conveying the CEO's request to meet with her at eight o'clock that morning.

Her daily routine shot, Katherine sank into her chair, trying to absorb the shock. That one request did more to frighten her than being reamed out by her boss. Was her job was at stake? What ever happened, her future was yet to be determined.

During her years of working for the oppressive Sandra Charney, senior vice president, corporate communications, Katherine had managed to keep out of Charney's way. By now she was accustomed to being isolated not only within her own department but from any contact with members of senior management. Her reward was to be left alone to handle her growing responsibilities. In all that time, she had never met the illusive Thomas Sweeney. Would this meeting change her future with the company, or give her boss a reason to fire her?

Thomas Sweeney had built the company from a local Midwest firm into a large corporation on the verge of becoming a public company. Known as the quality manufacturer of nutritionals and snack foods, Marathon produced popular health bars made from seaweed, grains and nuts, as well as nutritional supplements derived from a variety of herbs and food sources; some ingredients having been used by apothecaries in ancient China.

Waiting in the 40th floor reception area outside the inner sanctum of Marathon Nutritionals chief executive, Katherine sat on a stiff upholstered wing chair trying not to fidget. Her short blonde hair fell to just below her jaw, framing a peaches and cream complexion with a minimum of cosmetic enhancement. Fingering the collar of her silk blouse, she was the epitome of a young corporate executive.

"Ms. Cunningham, Mr. Sweeney will see you now," said Mrs. Tunney, the CEO's aide-de-camp and official gate keeper. A matronly woman of indeterminate age with a natural Irish charm, she reminded Katherine of a family retainer. Back straight, gray streaked hair combed in a neat off-the-face style and dressed in a suit lacking in feminine touches or frills of any kind. Mrs. Tunney could be formidable as she resolutely protected her boss, but had always been unfailingly polite and helpful whenever Katherine called to request information for a news release or speech she had been working on.

"Thank you, Mrs. Tunney, will there be anyone else joining us?"

"No, Ms. Cunningham. Go right in."

Keep calm. Don't fidget. Remember to smile, Katherine thought, as she entered the corner power suite, her clenched slightly damp hand holding a small leather folio. The room had a wall of windows dressed in heavy taupe drapery that accented the room's beige and brown furnishings. The morning sun added energy to the calm décor and seemed to light a path toward the dignified man standing beside his desk.

So this was Thomas Sweeney, the power behind Marathon Nutritionals. Trying not to stare, she was struck to find him the picture of elegance and far more handsome than his official photos. They were stiff, formal images, and this six-foot plus vision was anything but. Graying blond hair framed a face of sharp angles and planes, softened by a generous mouth turned slightly up at the corners in a smile of greeting. Sweeney's company bio said he was 60-years-old, but as a triathlete he had maintained the wiry frame of a man twenty years younger. Katherine was familiar with his athletic activities, especially his interest in the sport because it was her responsibility to prepare all materials for the company's Annual Sweeney Family Foundation Triathlon.

As Sweeney walked over and gave her hand a warm squeeze-like shake, Katherine unclenched her folio in relief. Whatever the reason for the meeting, she didn't feel she was about to lose her job.

With a slight wave of his hand, Sweeney indicated that Katherine should follow him to a seating area across the sunlit room. She noted his subdued demeanor, as if he were about to share a confidence. *How unexpected,* she thought. *He doesn't appear the fearsome dictator rumored by company gossips.*

"Ms. Cunningham I have wanted to meet you for some time. I am pleased you were able to join me at this early hour."

"I'm usually in early, Mr. Sweeney. Part of my responsibilities are to read the *New York Times* and *Wall Street Journal* before the start of our business day. In that way I can alert Sandra to any articles relevant to our industry. She is always on the lookout for a reporter searching for a qualified source for comment."

Settling his lean body in an adjacent chair, he nodded. "Ms. Cunningham, I have an out-of-the box situation. I am hoping it is something you can help me with."

Folding and refolding her hands that had been lying still on her lap, she thought, *this couldn't be happening.* Her silence echoed in her own ears.

"I realize that my requesting your assistance falls outside your normal responsibilities. Will that cause you any misgivings?"

While she considered Sweeney's business-like tone, she was taken with his sincerity.

"I am happy to be of assistance Mr. Sweeney, but wouldn't you prefer working with Ms. Charney when she returns from vacation? As you know she handles all assignments pertaining to senior management." She hoped he would take the hint. She could feel her boss's office temperature drop to subzero when she learned that Sweeney had personally asked her to handle a special assignment.

Paying close attention for any sign that Sweeney knew her predicament, Katherine was relieved to see the man's mischievous smile.

"I would not normally turn to you, however I believe you possess talents better suited to this situation. The truth is that I need someone outside of the normal channels of communications." While his tone was friendly, something in Sweeney's erect posture signified urgency.

"Thank you for your confidence," she replied, intrigued that Sweeney had implied he was aware of her work for the corporation. While her title was vice president corporate communications, Katherine was in fact Sandra Charney's underling, something made clear to her daily by the manner and dictates of her boss. She could hear her now, *Cunningham, how dare you defy me! You are never to speak to a member of senior management.*

Katherine's attention was diverted by thoughts of her first introduction to Marathon Nutritionals. It was during a nine month assignment as a graduate intern working for the assistant to the vice president of operations. It was then, as it was now, Mr. Sweeney's company. During her tenure she had gained a new respect for the oft maligned nutritional industry. Doubters believed that only FDA approved drugs should be used for treating health conditions. Working that semester at Marathon had changed her mind.

The company's New York City headquarters were in a soaring granite building erected in the 1930s. Its solid appearance signified strength, stability and success. She remembered being a gofer, filing, making copies, and entering data into the department's computerized spreadsheets. As basic as her work was, Katherine became acquainted with several of the newer Marathon products. She especially liked the fact the company didn't make outrageous claims of miracle cures. The packaging clearly stated the ingredients and the conditions they were developed to treat.

So upon graduating Columbia, with an MBA in communications, Katherine applied for an opening in the company's corporate communications department. Her graduate thesis on the educational importance of news releases had been cited by the human resources administrator as the main reason Sandra Charney had selected her from among four other candidates. Even though Katherine had some idea of the company's senior executive team, she had been unprepared for Charney's tight control over everyone in her group.

After years in bondage when I am about to quit, here comes an opportunity to bypass the Bitch. It's my one chance to stay with the company. Settling back in her cushioned chair, Katherine eagerly waited for Sweeney to continue.

"What I am about to share with you is highly sensitive and it requires the utmost discretion. First, can you work outside the normal procedures of your department? By that I mean that you would not be able to use the company's email system, office telephones, or have any written communication between us on your office computer. For the time being, everything must be handled with the utmost secrecy."

Shifting her position to gain time, Katherine's mind focused on his stated precautions. "Err, Mr. Sweeney, am I to understand that no one outside the two of us is to be aware of this project? That is, until I have your permission to convey specific information?"

"Correct. Don't misunderstand me Ms. Cunningham. Sandra has provided loyal and exemplary service to the company. However, let's say she is prone to get prickly if the media doesn't deliver to her satisfaction. That can't happen. The corporation's reputation and credibility with our customers, not to mention the Board of Directors, would be adversely affected."

Bless his heart. I think he understands.

"Ms. Cunningham, may I call you Katherine? I believe in using the first name of someone I am going to trust with the safety of my company.

"Of course, Mr. Sweeney."

"Good. You, young lady, have a skill for presenting information in clear concise manner that prevents it from being misconstrued or causing unneeded scrutiny by the FDA. My staff is in an ongoing dialogue with the FDA in an effort to keep off their radar. I, therefore, appreciate your reports on Marathon's research into Asian herbal formulas. Your work has showcased complicated anecdotal details without over promising on results. It is this direct style that will be most crucial now."

Katherine was surprised the CEO was actually citing some of her more complex assignments. A bit more comfortable, her mind returned to the problem at hand. Just what did this confidential project entail? And was she up to the task? "You have my attention and my promise to keep what you are about to divulge between the two of us."

Leaning forward and holding Katherine's gaze, he began, "We have a delicate situation that you and I must resolve, quietly and quickly. I feel your skills, understanding of the media and, let us say, feminine appeal, will go a long way in helping me avert a crisis that could have serious consequences for the company."

"Mr. Sweeney, thank you for your confidence in me." Katherine couldn't help responding to his subtle charm. He wasn't flirting but in the few minutes they had been speaking, he certainly had warmed in his manner towards her. He hadn't needed to butter her up in order to gain her allegiance. Simply knowing that she existed had won her over.

"Mr. Sweeney, I have learned a great deal working for Ms. Charney, and one thing I know how to do is work covertly. And, as you noted, I have a softer approach to working with others. I have my own laptop and when necessary, can access office files from home. I also have a smart phone for calls and a private email account. That should take care of things nicely."

"Don't underestimate Sandra. I am sure if she suspects something out of the ordinary, she will, and can, track down all access to company information. If I have learned anything recently, nothing in a computer is sacrosanct."

Katherine watched as Sweeney unfolded his six foot plus figure and walked over to his desk. His movements exhibited the control of well-conditioned muscles. Returning with a slim file, he handed it to her with a look of resignation.

"The bottom-line is that Edward Abbott has just resigned as chief financial officer. The reasons are personal, but in fairness to you, and with your assurance of secrecy, I will share them." She nodded in agreement wondering what could cause Abbott's resignation that would be serious enough for secrecy.

"Katherine, you are not to disclose this information. While I do not expect you to lie, especially to the press, unless the circumstances behind his resignation come to light, it isn't to be discussed. Do we understand one another?" His gray eyes drilled home the gravity of his instructions.

Clearing her throat, she nodded, waiting for him to continue. Sweeney did say she didn't have to lie. Regardless of the widely held belief that everyone in public relations lied, she never had, even when Sandra had wanted her to rephrase a news release to imply that a new supplement was being submitted to the FDA for approval. While there were liars in all professions, she didn't operate that way.

"All right then." Sweeney settled back in his chair. "Mr. Abbott is the husband of my niece Megan. While she married him after meeting him here, he is still family. Anything untoward by him leaves Marathon open to charges of nepotism. I learned yesterday that Mr. Abbott is being blackmailed. He personally tendered his resignation to me and explained that he had embezzled $800,000 from the Sweeney Family Foundation to pay off the blackmailer. He could no longer live with the knowledge of his actions. Greatly shamed, he vowed to help recover the funds and be available any way necessary to answer for his betrayal to me and the company."

"Excuse me Mr. Sweeney, why was he being blackmailed? Can he restore the funds without being detected? Have you alerted law enforcement officials?" She had many more questions, but the look on Sweeney's face halted her mid thought. *Why is he smiling?*

"One thing at a time, Katherine. I knew you were the right person for this task."

Returning to the business at hand, he continued, "Edward knows that if this blackmailer were to disclose his actions, it would damage his reputation of being the conscientious keeper of Marathon's financial affairs. He would also be prosecuted for theft. If that were to happen, Marathon would be subject to destructive investigations and accompanying onslaught by the media. The public could possibly lose faith in our products and we would be unable to continue on our path towards listing Marathon Nutritionals on the stock exchange." Sweeney paused, then looked directly at her. "And, no, I haven't notified anyone about this crisis, outside of you."

This certainly wasn't what Katherine had expected. Outside of Sweeney himself, Edward Abbott was by reputation the most correct, honorable, and hard-working man in the company. While she hadn't worked directly with him, she had read interviews he had given and was impressed by his carefully considered responses. In addition to his position as chief financial officer, he served as one of three Directors of the Sweeney Family Foundation that funded outreach programs to improve health conditions in rural areas of the country.

Being forbidden from working with senior management, Katherine's only memory of seeing Mr. Abbott was when she was instructed to take notes at a company meeting and then write it up for a company report. Seated in the back of the conference room, she listened as he presented Marathon's activities during the previous period. In precise language he explained how the company was working towards encouraging use of holistic methods for eliminating common childhood infections and diseases. Now she wondered how a man of his character, who guarded his every word, could be blackmailed.

Just jump in. "This project is to be covert, and above all else, avoid creating a media frenzy. Am I correct?"

"Precisely! The way I see it, we will need a news release announcing Edward's resignation. It should include a review of his contributions to the organization, maybe mention his charitable work. But in no way, should it refer to the missing funds or that he is married to my niece. Do you have any thoughts as to how this might be accomplished?"

Taking a moment to review the information in the folder, Katherine knew that a too brief announcement would raise questions. A densely-worded release would cause close scrutiny. "Mr. Sweeney, let me draft an approach and we can meet again to fill in the details. I will need specifics including a listing of Mr. Abbott's accomplishments and information pertaining to his charitable work. But I think we could say he was resigning at a time when the company was on a safe course of growth to pursue personal interests. Maybe he could be setting up an organization to help seriously ill children in rural America. Something like that, but it should be an offshoot of his current charitable interests."

"Yes, I agree. I can have Mrs. Tunney provide you with the information. She will deliver it into your hands within the hour."

"Another thing, if we could have Mr. Abbott interviewed by one or two carefully selected business reporters it could forestall questions about the reason behind his early retirement. It would show that he had nothing to hide. Can he be available? More importantly, will he be able to handle an interview without appearing to be hiding something?"

"I see you understand your audience. Let me talk with Edward. Then with his input, we will be able to develop our strategy. Let's say the three of us meet tomorrow evening in the privacy of my home. Katherine, you might come prepared with some hard-hitting questions. Edward will want to be prepared for the very worst."

"Of course. Will you be naming his successor?"

"I will, however, I haven't as yet spoken to him. I should have an answer for you tomorrow evening. Let's say 7 pm."

"Good. That will complete the story on this change of corporate officers. Another thing, you should probably time the announcement for release after 4 pm this Friday. That way the company won't be immediately approached for additional comment. This is a standard practice of public companies when issuing potentially sensitive information and not wanting it to have an immediate impact the price of their stock."

"Of course, Katherine, we aren't a public company yet, so Marathon shouldn't be on anyone's watch list, especially the SECs. But, you are correct. It is better to be safe."

"Let me rough out a draft and bring it by around five this afternoon for your comments."

"I think we will work very well together. And, Katherine, if we can have most of the post announcement pieces in place by the weekend, Sandra won't have to become involved. I will brief Sandra on the need to rush this announcement and that I asked you to handle it in her absence. That by having you work with the media, it would be received as being of no material importance to the company's normal business operations."

Katherine's mind was a buzz. *Right, my being involved is of little importance. To the media, maybe, but not to me. For all the time I've worked for Charney she has been the only one to work directly with the media. No matter how extensive my research, the information was always sent from the desk of Sandra Charney, Sr. VP Communications. The Bitch is going to have kittens, or maybe that should be puppies when she hears of this!*

"Thank you Mr. Sweeney…for understanding my situation." As Katherine rose to leave she had all she could do to keep from kissing this sensitive man. He seemed to understand by requesting her assistance he might be inviting problems for her from her boss.

Dismissed to begin her assignment, Katherine headed to her office two floors below, steeling herself in readiness for the week's activities. Not only was she to assist with a top secret mission, she knew when Sandra Charney returned from vacation, her life was going to be a perfect storm.

2

Katherine's first activity of the day was to check her emails for anything that required immediate attention. Noticing one from Sandra, she held her breath. *She hasn't been out of the office one day and she's sending me emails?* Opening the message she read:

> Cunningham – I want you to make up a list of reporters we can contact for one-on-one interviews with key members of our research team. It won't be a long list, but I also want samples of their articles covering nutritional products. I am only targeting major business print media, not the trade press. Messenger all relevant materials to my home by end of business Friday.
>
> S C

"Yes Madam! I can't contact you, but you can send me work! Why am I not surprised?" Katherine whispered her retorts. She had learned the hard way that Charney had eyes and ears of unknown spies to inform her of the smallest infraction by one of her staff. If she hadn't known better, Katherine would have accused her boss of having bugged her office. Now she wondered at something Sweeney had said about nothing on computers being sacrosanct. If she was getting new assignments from her vacationing boss while handling Sweeney's crisis, she had to triple check everything. Any mix-up between assignments would be devastating.

Pulling out her mini laptop from her tote bag, Katherine began structuring the Abbott announcement. Form over content is what was needed.

The day flew by. Fortunately it was only Monday, giving her four days to complete Charney's request. Removing a flash drive containing a copy of the Abbott draft from her laptop, she pocketed it and headed for Sweeney's office. Seeing his door closed, she looked at Mrs. Tunney.

"I have information on this flash drive for Mr. Sweeney. Under the circumstances, it wasn't possible for me to print the document downstairs."

"One moment please." Mrs. Tunney picked up her phone and conveyed the information to her boss. "Yes, Mr. Sweeney. I'll print the document for your changes."

Katherine handed her the small seemingly innocent bit of technology. "Should I wait or stop by first thing in the morning?"

"Why not go back to your office and I'll call your cell shortly. However, my guess is that Mr. Sweeney will have some changes, and if you stop by early tomorrow you can pick them up."

That was perfectly acceptable to Katherine. She wasn't in any hurry. She would need considerably more information than she had included in the brief page and a half draft. At least she could be assured that no one outside of Sweeney, Tunney, and herself would know the contents on the memory stick.

Back at her desk, she took out a notepad and began to frame questions for her meeting with Abbott and Sweeney. Just what was he being blackmailed for? How did he transfer that large amount of money without alerting anyone at the Sweeney Family Foundation? Why only $800,000 and not $1 million? Did he have any idea who was blackmailing him? Once she had framed her questions, Katherine entered them into a secure file on her laptop and destroyed her hand written notes.

As expected, Mrs. Tunney called an hour later to let her know she should stop by the office in the morning and if Mr. Sweeney had anything to add he would tell her then.

It was after seven when Katherine called it a day. She picked up her cell and called Sally, her best friend from college. She needed to decompress over a martini at the neighborhood watering hole.

"Ready to pack it in?" she asked. "I could really use a drink and your cheerful reminder that there is a life outside our careers." Getting an earful about being too serious, Katherine hung up, turned off her computer, stuffed her laptop into her tote bag, grabbed her handbag and pulled on her coat. It wasn't just the martini she needed, she wanted Sally's legal mind to help her deal with this new development in her career.

*   *   *

Sally's law firm was headquartered a couple of blocks north on Park Avenue. While there were several cocktail lounges and after-hours bars in the neighborhood, Katherine and Sally preferred to meet in local spots on the upper Eastside of Manhattan, an area closer to their apartments. One of their favorites was Malachy's, a dimly lit establishment on a small intimate scale. New York featured an Irish pub on almost every block, but unlike some in their neighborhood, Malachy's had booths instead of just open table seating. Since Katherine and Sally usually discussed some problem related to their careers, they preferred the privacy afforded by Malachy's.

"So ladies," greeted Michael, their usual waiter. "What can I get you tonight?"

Looking at Sally, Katherine piped up, "A vodka martini with three olives, straight up."

"Make that two," Sally added.

"Right-o, ladies. Coming up."

"Don't just sit there waiting for a drink. Give. Things must be bad not to order your usual red wine."

"Sally, give me a minute to calm down. I'm going to need a drink before I begin my tale of woe."

When Michael set down their drinks, Katherine nodded him her thanks, watching as he turned back towards the bar. Practically inhaling her first sip, Katherine looked across the table to her friend, her spine now stiffened by vodka. "I am either going to finally get away from the Bitch or, the Bitch will push me over the proverbial cliff."

"Isn't she on vacation somewhere warm? How can she fire you long distance?"

Sally had been her friend since her graduate days at Columbia. While Sally was in the law school, Katherine was in the school of journalism. Thinking back to end of exams, any exam, Katherine remembered joining Sally at her dorm room and together they'd mix up a batch of drinks. Relieved that another round of tests were over they'd indulge in their favorite topic – men. What they wanted in a date. Who would marry first and other dreams of young women yet to make their mark on the world. Their bond of friendship had survived the ups and downs in each of their lives. Katherine knew that whatever she told Sally would go no further. But this wasn't the usual office gossip. It was her career.

"Sally, this is top secret. Swear not to breathe even a hint of what I'm going to tell you?"

"Sure. But, if you can't divulge certain details, my legal advice, as your personal attorney, is not to. Just tell me what's got you in Sandra's killing zone."

"I was called into a meeting with the CEO, Thomas Sweeney. And, I'm not to let the Bitch know anything about it. That means working in secret because working in routine fashion would certainly be spotted by one of her spies."

"And, knowing just how paranoid she is, when she returns you'd be toast," Sally concluded.

Nodding, Katherine allowed the next sip of her martini to coat the inside of her mouth before swallowing and warming her chilled body. "I've given her my all for seven years and she treats me like a lowly intern." Mimicking the crisp cold voice of her boss, Katherine said, "Ms. Cunningham, never release anything without my signature. You are not to use the executive elevator. And never meet with a department head without speaking to me first."

Taking another sip of her drink, she continued, "For seven years, I've worked my ass off for that woman. Last night fueled with a bottle of red wine, I decided I'm at a dead end. I have to leave and look for another position. Maybe this time I should move to a PR agency." Having finished her tirade she, sipped her drink and waited for one of Sally's on target follow-ups.

"Can you handle this assignment? Do you want to take the risk? Is it worth incurring Charney's ire?"

"Yes, Yes and Yes."

"So what's the problem? You just told me that you were thinking of quitting. That you'd had it. We've had this conversation before and you said that no salary was worth living in a state of angst."

"I only decided to quit last night." Then looking at her friend, a sudden change in mood animating her features, she said. "Now I dream of working for a man I'd never met. He's human, bright, engages your mind and engenders loyalty. What a refreshing change that will be."

Sally signaled Michael for another round.

"I really shouldn't have another. I haven't eaten anything since a bagel at ten this morning."

"This is an occasion. As your legal advisor, I am instructing you to play things close to your chest. You're smart, handle the most sensitive situations with delicacy of a born diplomat, and when it comes to planning, you're as precise as a military field commander. Remember how you planned out the entire company meeting, making sure that each of the VPs spent no more than eight minutes delivering their presentations without boring their audience? If memory serves, you wrote their speeches and prepared their accompanying slides. Didn't you tell me that Sandra hadn't had even one complaint?"

Thinking about Sally's comment, Katherine thought that Charney rarely complained about her work. Tongue lashing was almost always used when she had forgotten one of Charney's strict rules. Savoring the memory of that meeting, Katherine's thought once again, here was proof she was good at her job.

When Michael returned with their drinks, Sally changed the subject. "So Michael, how's your book coming? When can I read a draft? After all, you have been drilling me for over a year about how a devious businessman can get away with his illegal machinations."

New York City waiters and waitresses were either actors waiting for a break, or novelists seeking an agent. Michael not only served as their waiter, he was also an unofficial friend. As a writer, yet to make his mark with a bestselling novel, Michael often tried out one of his plot problems on Katherine and Sally.

"So what's it like in corporate America now that everything is online?" he asked.

"Michael, just what do you want me to tell you? You know our computer and phone systems are protected by multiple firewalls. If we don't keep updating our security systems, everything we sent online could be broadcast to the world."

"For all your smarts and sass you can't make me believe the corporate club is as inviolate as it professes."

"Michael, stop tweaking Sally. I read excerpts from your last manuscript, and it included more internet treachery than I knew was possible." Laughing at his attempt to spark a debate helped Katherine relax a bit more, alcohol was doing the rest.

"Enough you two. Michael, I'd better order before Sally has to carry me home. So, I'll have a burger rare with two slices of raw onion and sweet potato fries."

"Sounds good to me, but hold the onions," Sally added. Both women watched Michael walk away. "Hey girlfriend, there goes a fabulous man. Why not act like you were interested the next time he stops by the table?" Sally asked.

"He is rather a spectacular specimen, sensitive, friendly and understands the pressures of our careers. I guess I never thought about him in that way."

"Speaking of men, when was the last time you had a sweaty time in bed?"

Choking on a sip of her drink, Katherine responded with a laugh. "About two years ago when I last saw Noel."

"Yeah. Remind me why you have stopped seeing that cad?"

"You know why. I couldn't take it anymore. In two years, I never met even one of his friends, we never took a trip or spent a weekend together. In fact, I never spent an entire night with the man. It wasn't a relationship. It was hooking up."

"Have you even thought about dating? Trying an online service? I've met some interesting men online. I haven't found my perfect guy, but at least I'm out there trying."

"Oh Sally, I loved him too much. Maybe if I hadn't I would have tried to find someone else. A man who wanted to spend all of his free time with me."

"I kept trying to fix you up but you always had some excuse. Noel said he'd call. Or, you had too much work. As if I didn't have another brief to draft."

"I gave up on him, and now talking to you I realize I really gave up on myself. Anyway when would I have time to date? I can just see myself with some dreamy guy at a restaurant about to cut into my steak when the Bitch rings my cell demanding an answer to some minor detail. Something I'd have to return to the office, open my files and look up. That would scotch any budding relationship. No matter how understanding the guy was, the possibility of anything developing would be cut short before it had a chance. I'd never hear from him again."

"If you keep eating raw onions, you won't have to worry about it."

3

Megan was shocked to find her husband of six years sitting in a trance facing the book-lined wall behind his orderly desk. The den was a place her husband cherished. He had designed every nook and tech feature in their classic six Eastside New York apartment, and this one room was his sanctuary. He never just sat there with a blank look on his dark, handsome features. Usually, when she passed by she'd pause to watch Edward's animated face as he sat immersed in a book or working out a crossword puzzle. She knew if left on his own, Edward would spend all of his out of office hours in this, his favorite place. He told her once that growing up in a family with four kids hadn't given him any privacy. In this room he could free his mind for exploring new adventures. In addition to his collection of books, he had built-in all the tech toys he needed for the music, video and computer games he so loved.

"Sweetheart?" Megan's soft voice preceded her into the quiet room. "I was on my way to get a cup of tea and wondered if you'd like one?" Standing by the desk, she waited for even a flicker of a response.

"Edward?" Breathing a little easier as the face of the man she loved slowly come back to life, Megan saw a deep melancholy, a hollowness of expression, and it scared her. The man she had lived with for six years was the most even-tempered, confident person she'd ever met. Outside of her Uncle Thomas, there was no one she loved more on this earth.

"Dear, aren't you going into the office this morning? Or did you finally listen to me and take a day off?" Usually her light banter brought Edward out of one of his rare moods.

"What?"

Even his voice was sad. Hiding behind a cajoling smile, Megan placed a gentle hand on her husband's shoulder and was relieved to see her touch had brought a glimmer of life back into his face. "Where were you just now?"

Blinking, Edward began rubbing his eyes, "Lost."

"Are you ill? Should I call the doctor?" Getting no response, Megan knew she had to shake him out of his daze. "Sweetheart, is there something you can talk over with me? Maybe I can help."

With a heart breaking sigh, Edward reached out to his wife and, understanding his need, Megan hugged him close. "Whatever is wrong, we can get through it sweetheart." Taking his face in her hands, Megan kissed him, her tenderness causing tears.

"Why not tell me what's bothering you? Keeping problems to ourselves, only lets us see one side of things."

Edward reached up and pulled her onto his lap. Megan snuggled close feeling him wrap her in an embrace. With his head resting on her shoulder, he uttered a soul searing groan. "Love, we have to talk." Rising, with Megan's hand in his, he led her to the sofa. Remaining standing, shoulders slumped and eyes focused on his shoes, Edward turned away and began to slowly pace around the room.

Megan knew her husband's thoughts once again turned inward. She remained silent, not wanting to intrude, and prayed she would be able to find a solution to whatever had created Edward's morose mood.

How lucky she was to have met this loving man. The ten year difference in their ages hadn't been an impediment to building a life together. Her only regret was she hadn't given her husband the child they both wanted. Megan had lost her parents when she was only seven and was raised by her father's older brother, Uncle Thomas. Thomas had lost his wife to cancer early in his marriage and raised Megan as the child he never had. Megan wanted a child to build a family of her own and have Uncle Thomas share her joy. An infant they could watch grow, to love and nurture, filling a hole in both of their lives.

Jolted out of her reverie by Edward sitting down next to her, Megan waited, determined to help resolve whatever had caused his perplexing mood.

Picking up both of his wife's hands, Edward gave them a gentle squeeze. "I went to see Thomas yesterday and gave him my resignation. He was very kind. Understanding in fact. I didn't deserve that."

Resign? He loved his job. Megan knew that to keep her husband talking, she couldn't bombard him with questions. Getting Edward to talk about anything required patience. He unrolled each word as if unraveling a string of Christmas lights.

"I also told him that I had stolen $800,000 from the Foundation. And this is the hard part, telling him why. Next to confessing my sins to you, admitting my theft to him was the hardest thing I've ever done."

"Do we need money? Eight hundred thousand dollars' worth? Of course we must repay it." Megan was stunned. While they were comfortable financially, it would take everything they had to help Edward return the funds. "I know we can sell the apartment. Even with the mortgage we can get something. Can't we?"

Thinking back to the purchase of their condominium, she remembered the visits they had with the architect and interior designer. Each had a wish list of features they wanted built into their new home. She had designed her dream kitchen and of course had each of the fifteen closets outfitted with custom cabinets and shelves. Smiling, she remembered watching her husband standing over the floor plans with the architect discussing moving a wall, or specifying wiring sufficient to power a computerized home control system. She told Edward she hadn't needed window shades that could be raised and lowered with the flip of a switch. And they certainly didn't need a home theater, that a television mounted on a wall in the den would be sufficient. But Edward hadn't listened. Instead he had installed a screen that could be lowered behind his desk when they stayed home to watch a newly rented film. Worried about her safety, when she was at home without him, Edward had also specified that the architect include the latest home security system.

Totaling the construction costs to update the prewar apartment, and all the custom furnishings they had purchased, Megan realized they had spent a small fortune. She also knew they had paid for these expenses by seriously depleting their retirement accounts and the rest with withdrawals from their individual investment portfolios. She doubted if they had enough assets remaining to restore all of the $800,000 Edward had taken from the Foundation.

"I am afraid there's more." Resuming his pacing around the room, he took his time before continuing. To her surprise, when Edward stopped his roaming he knelt in front of her, enfolding both her hands in his and looked directly into her face. "I am being blackmailed," he whispered. "The blackmailer sent me a video. It pictures me in bed with a young woman. I don't remember how I got there or know who she was. All I know is that somehow I was tricked, and to prevent the video from being made public, I had to give this thief, $800,000."

Pulling free of Edward's grasp, she cried, "You cheated on me?" Her strangled retort came from her gut. "After all we have been to each other, you threw it away?" Megan jumped to her feet, pushing her husband off balance, he lay sprawled on the carpet. "Is this something new or have you been cheating on me all along?" This is the man she swore to love forever. It wasn't real. It couldn't be. Unaware of the shame and sorrow on Edwards face, all Megan could see was the shattering of her faith in a man she loved beyond reason.

"All those nights you worked late. Were they a lie as well?" With tears streaming, Megan covered her face with her hands. As her mind raged, her body absorbed the shock. She couldn't reconcile what she heard with the man she thought she knew.

Edward moved closer and wrapped her in his arms, then joined her in tears.

When her shaking stopped, Megan pulled away and looked her husband in the eyes. She saw the shell of a man, beaten by actions foreign to his very nature. It was then Megan felt something off kilter. The Edward she loved couldn't have done any of the things he just described. Theft? Taking another woman to bed? There had to be something he wasn't telling her.

Her voice a mere whisper, she asked, "You don't know who this woman is, this thief?"

"No. I have tried to retrace my steps and can't connect that video to anything I remember."

When Megan first met Edward, she was struck by his unswerving loyalty to Thomas, and then as they became involved, he committed himself completely to her and their life together. He was the personification of honor. The seeds of doubt softened her anger, and she began to question not only the problem, but her faith in her husband. Could he? Would he? Had he cheated?

"Darling, you are my life. I don't know how I got myself into this situation," he pleaded. "You know I wouldn't do anything to hurt you, and I certainly wouldn't steal from Thomas."

Megan dropped back down on the sofa. She had always relied on her internal compass to tell her truth from lies. Why wasn't she listening now? Living as man and wife for six years, Megan knew Edward wasn't a man who would steal from Thomas, and he certainly wouldn't do anything to harm her. It wasn't who he was. The realization eased some of her fears. Then the fears returned as she thought about the lengths Edward had to go to, both literally and morally, to meet the blackmailer's demands. Money was one thing, but blackmail over a falsely created affair? That was a criminal act.

Grabbing her husband in a tight hug, Megan reminded herself this is the man she fell in love with. "Edward, listen to me. I love and trust you. If you say you were set-up, then I am going to help you find out why. No, don't say you'll handle it alone…that you're trying to protect me. I couldn't stand that. We're a team."

Seeing the shell of the man she so loved once again break into tears tore her apart. Megan needed to remain strong, determined find the truth and clear his name. First she'd have to restore Edward's ability to remember that fateful day. Then together do whatever they could to track the blackmailer.

4

The soft breezes lulled Sandra Charney into a somnolent state of bliss. This was the relief she needed. No responsibilities. No one looking over her shoulder or second guessing her decisions. Why couldn't she work alone? Not worry about someone younger pushing her out of her job.

Her life was perfectly planned. She earned her position at Marathon through long hours, hard work and having no personal life. This vacation was one of her rewards. A decadent escape from day-to-day reality. Another, her growing investment portfolio. She had met Geoffrey Lockwood during a vacation in Tenerife more than a decade ago. During a conversation over dinner, he had introduced her to the shadowy world of international investing. When he told her she could participate in small but lucrative international real estate transactions, her dreams of wealth seemed almost in reach. Hard work only got her a six-figure income. Not enough to fill a life-long greed born of humble beginnings. After having Lockwood checked out by a local detective-for-hire, she had given him $10,000 of her hard earned savings. Lockwood turned out to be a genus, having turned that initial investment, along with small subsequent additions, into several millions.

Sandra felt the knots in her shoulders and back begin to unkink as Maria, massaging fragrant coconut oil into her skin, was eliciting a series of contented murmurs. As the masseuse continued her kneading and smoothing strokes, Sandra considered the man she saw the night before in the terrace dining room. The hotel was small and exclusive, having fewer than twenty individual bungalows and a main building with fifty rooms for guests. Sandra chose this particular destination because previous favorite getaway locations had become entirely too popular. She couldn't afford to be spotted by anyone from her regular world. To those in her professional life, Sandra was the pristine symbol of a cool, crisp and impersonal businesswoman. Not the temptress she became during her week-long runaways from reality.

The stranger had caught her eye during the flight from Fiji to Turtle Island. She had been so tired it wasn't until she had rested and eaten a light dinner that she could even begin to think about the lean man, tall and straight, possibly with a military background. Smiling as she conjured up images of wild hours of passion with someone she would never see after her weeks' vacation, Sandra began plotting a meaningful introduction. Yes, for now, a Turtle Island bungalow would be her Nirvana.

*　　　*　　　*

The sun was beginning its colorful descent over the ocean when Sandra, dressed in a shimmering column of sky blue silk chiffon, strolled over to the bar and perched on a high stool next to the object of her morning's musings. Ordering a sidecar straight up and sensing the change in posture of the quiet stranger, she glanced down and to her left, not wanting to stare. Noticing that his hands were ring-free and had the manicured elegance of a gentleman, Sandra slowly looked up into a sun-creased face.

"Do you paint?" she asked in soft husky tones barely loud enough to be heard. She had heard him chuckle and thought that this was a promising beginning. Sandra didn't believe in coincidences, not in her social life and certainly not her professional one.

Leaning closer to hear her almost whispered question, the man smiled. "Not with paints. I'm sorry, weren't you on the plane coming over from the mainland?"

"Yes, and I am afraid I wasn't very sociable. It had been a long day and I needed a bath and sleep."

Holding out his hand, and looking slightly amused, he replied in promising tones, "I'm Ian, and I am very glad you are joining society here at Turtle Bay." He lifted Sandra's be-ringed hand to his lips, and she felt his breath before his lips lightly brushed and then kissed her palm. "I'm happy to meet you on more friendly terms."

Oh he is delicious. Is that a faint Scottish burr I hear under that polished voice?

"Sandra." Looking up into Ian's deep green eyes, she saw a twinkle that promised delightfully intimate hours ahead. "If you don't use paint, are you in another artistic field?" she asked. Her voice was as smooth as the revitalized skin of her brow.

"Words. I paint with words."

That was suitably vague. Did he write fiction, non-fiction, poetry or annual reports? she wondered. "Isn't this a small world? I work with words as well."

"Words are sometimes over rated, don't you think?"

She found Ian's playful response encouraging. "Especially, Ian, if that is the way one earns a living. Are you taking a long break?"

"You could say I am on leave for my health. My spirit was lacking energy."

"Interesting. I'm actually taking a mental health break myself. You, however, don't look like you lost anything." Sandra was now practically in Ian's lap, close enough to smell his orange-scented after shave lotion.

"I may be getting it back. If I do, how may I thank you?"

Smiling her most seductively, Sandra winked. Words, she decided, would be a mistake. Why change the mood? She found Ian's chuckle at her silence so very sexy. And yes, he was good with words. What else would he be good at?

Sandra was enjoying the hum of back and forth between a man and woman sizing one another up for a possible connection. She noticed Ian only provided enough information in his creative answers to keep their repartee going. Under the impeccably dressed man, who could model sportswear for the International set, had to be an interesting story. It was too bad she wouldn't be delving more deeply. Finding out how this delicious specimen managed to be at Turtle Island had to be a story worth exploring. That, however, would only create complications when she said her farewells.

"Would you care to join me for dinner on the terrace? We could continue this delightful conversation, and who knows, follow dinner by a sinful dessert?" he asked.

Sandra sipped the last of her drink. Smiling, with the lusty promise of enjoying his suggestions, she rose. "Dessert is my favorite course."

*   *   *

The air in her bungalow shimmered with body heat and breezes from the ocean not more than fifty feet from the thatched roof building. Sandra lifted her head and took in the length of Ian's body as she ran a finger over his thigh, moving slowly up toward the curve where it merged with his hip. Pausing in her tactile journey, she felt the sleeping Adonis stir. "I didn't want to wake you, but your body called to me."

Rolling over to cover her body with his, Ian wore a sleepy smile that kindled a welcomed response. "My Lady seems restless. I wonder just how I might calm that spirit without crushing her enthusiasm."

As Ian began to nibble on Sandra's bottom lip, he moved his body so that it covered every inch of her skin. If skin was the body's largest organ, then he was certainly in touch with a remarkable amount of hers. With a patience she wasn't accustomed to practicing, Sandra closed her eyes to feel Ian's every nibbling move from her lips, to her neck, followed by his suckling a nipple on first one, then the other of her ample breasts.

For a woman of fifty, Sandra had taken advantage of modern cosmetic science to enhance and preserve her five foot two inch body. Her yearly escapes to Europe for cellular injections to keep her body youthful, along with her monthly visits to her dermatologist for cosmetic peels, and daily workouts with a personal trainer, enabled Sandra to forestall an aged-wrinkled and sagging body.

Ian's breath, now focused on her ear, had broken Sandra's control. Without separating her body from his, she seductively entwined herself around Ian until it was as if a magnet had mated them in place. Her movements rushed Ian to match her energy and shortly, breathlessly, mindlessly, she was heavenly spent.

"Mm...this is the most relaxed I've been in three years. Sandra, you are a wonder."

"My pleasure. I couldn't have done it without you."

"Are you always this spontaneous? Or does this island bring it out in you?"

Laughing almost to herself she thought, *If, he only knew.* "Actually I'm just visiting spontaneity. It's your influence."

Not wanting to continue the conversation, Sandra sat up and suggested they go for a midnight swim.

"Wonderful. But no bathing suits. I want to see every inch of that taught body in the moonlight." She was only too ready. All her dieting, purging, and strict exercise regimen had paid off. Grabbing for a beach towel hanging on the bedroom door, Sandra wrapped herself sarong style and rushed laughing out the bungalow door. Ian quickly followed, and lifting her off her feet, tossed her over his shoulder carrying her into the gentle moonlit surf.

5

The tension was beginning to show with Katherine's hair a limp helmet and her makeup badly in need of repair. It had been a full day finalizing the information she would need for the evening work session with Sweeney and Abbott. Desperate for a break, she headed downstairs for a cup of coffee to fuel her mind and body. It was her usual 4 pm Starbuck's run, but today it was a medicinal infusion.

Sipping her coffee, Katherine reviewed her media plan, pleased to have Sweeney's approval to approach the three reporters on her wish list. She had identified Sara Forman of CNN, Brian Harlin of *The Wall Street Journal,* and John Brawley of *Time.* All three were known to be fair minded. The results would announce Abbott's resignation to audiences of one cable news program, a daily business newspaper, and a weekly news magazine, thereby sharing the announcement with the public in a limited and controlled manner. It was well known that Marathon was reluctant to make its executives available for interviews.

Obtaining one with the retiring CFO of would be catnip, too good for them not to play ball.

Katherine didn't know what she would learn when she met with Mr. Abbott and heard his side of the story. Her draft of the announcement was straight forward, waiting for additional bits of information including the name and background of Abbott's successor. It was only Tuesday, giving her time to adjust her plan to accommodate new details essential to the final announcement.

While heading home early to get ready for the 7 pm meeting, Katherine had a niggling thought that something wasn't quite right. It wasn't until she entered her apartment she finally pegged the problem. She had left a notepad in her desk, and while that wasn't something she would normally worry about, it contained notes on Abbott's personal history. Mentally reviewing the entries, she thought that they were innocuous--dates on his marriage to Megan, quotes from his college yearbook profile, the year of his graduation from law school, an overview of his employment history with Marathon, and his current charitable works.

Sure it wouldn't tip her hand, Katherine threw her attention into dressing for the meeting. A bath, fresh makeup, and simple black cocktail dress would serve. It was a black crepe by Vera Wang and had cost her almost two week's salary. But it was designed to fit every business occasion, especially one of this gravity.

Turning to view the back of her dress in the mirror, Katherine was glad she had been too busy to eat. Her profile was slim, not a bulge to be found at her waist. This was the result of two days of stress. *Don't slump, shoulder's back, head up.* Her reflection showed a composed executive ready for an evening of serious business.

As she left her apartment, she knew being invited to the CEOs home was quite out of the ordinary. Katherine wondered if Charney had ever received an invitation. If not, she could picture her boss going into one of her fits when she found out Katherine had been so honored.

*   *   *

The taxi dropped Katherine off in front of a granite block, four story townhouse on upper Fifth Avenue. The iron portico was lit by coach lamps on either side of the shiny black door, creating a warm halo of light. Straightening her slim fitting cocktail dress under her wool coat, Katherine rang the bell and heard the echo of chimes inside the building.

"Ms. Cunningham, Mr. Sweeney is expecting you," said an older man dressed in a dark business suit. He took her coat and led her to a door off the main hall. Leaning down to the polished pewter door handle, he opened it to a wood lined room anchored by richly patterned carpets. Sweeney and Abbott stood in welcome as she entered the room. She was surprised to see Mrs. Abbott was also in the room and was pleased to find there were apparently no secrets in this family. The question was would they keep secrets from her?

Katherine had met Megan Abbott when she interned at Marathon more than eight years before. Megan, as she knew the woman, had been eminently more agreeable than her boss, Victor Rosso, the chief operating officer, and Katherine sought her assistance whenever possible. This woman was eight years older, stunningly attired in a simple cocktail dress, a dress with no apologies to Vera Wang, still made Katherine feel like a poor relation.

"Katherine, I would like to introduce you to Megan Abbott," Sweeney said as he approached with Mrs. Abbott on his arm. "It will be important for her to understand our strategy for announcing Edward's resignation." Hearing a note of protectiveness in his voice, Katherine remembered him telling her that Megan Abbott was his niece. When she had worked with this woman several years before, the relationship with Marathon's CEO had never been mentioned by Megan or anyone in their department.

As Katherine shook Mrs. Abbott's hand, she was struck with a genuine feeling of sympathy. She was obviously in love with her husband. It wasn't anything she said, it was more a softness of expression when she looked his way.

"It is a pleasure to meet you again. You were very kind to me as a young intern. Never too busy to answer one of my many questions. And, if I remember correctly, prior to your working at Marathon you were an account executive with a public relations agency. That will be invaluable as we work through this announcement." When Katherine saw her small smile, she realized Mrs.

Abbott also remembered their shared experiences, and was now a bit more comfortable under these difficult circumstances. Looking over to Sweeney, Katherine saw him nod his approval.

Katherine sat on a nearby wing chair and opened a slim folio. She pulled out copies of the news release, along with information about the three reporters she had identified to interview Edward Abbott. "This material will give you an idea of what each reporter will be looking for." Waiting for Edward to read a draft of the news release, Katherine noted the intensity with which Mrs. Abbott reviewed samples of the reporter's articles. *So much for the wife as a shadow,* Katherine thought.

"Katherine, I think we can all agree with your choices in journalists, but are you sure they will agree to an interview with only a few hours of notice?" Sweeney asked.

"Yes, sir. I plan to call them late Thursday afternoon, and once they agree to embargo the news release and interview until after four o'clock the next day, I will schedule phone conferences with Mr. Abbott and myself for Friday. If a reporter wishes to stop by, we will accommodate him or her. If we are lucky, they will be more than happy with a telephone exclusive."

"Might I suggest a teleconferenced interview?" Mrs. Abbott interjected. "That way, Edward will appear not to be hiding anything."

"Another possibility for us to consider." Turning to Edward Abbott, Katherine asked, "Mr. Abbott, will you be comfortable on camera?"

"I think so. My usual manner is rather formal and my answers brief. These particular reporters will be expecting that."

"Edward, dear, Ms. Cunningham will be there and can address any unexpected cross directs by the reporters." Megan's encouragement was accepted and with a slight smile, and he turned his attention back to Katherine.

"We should, however, be prepared for difficult questions." Looking at Sweeney, Katherine continued with her briefing. "One of the needed pieces to this announcement is missing. I should also have the name and background of Mr. Abbotts' successor, his qualifications, and history with the company...or, with his previous employer."

"Edward agrees with me in elevating his longtime assistant, Gregory Pomeroy, to chief financial officer. I have spoken with Greg, and he is pleased to learn that the reason behind his promotion is simply that Edward has chosen to retire and recommended him for the position. I am confident that if needed we have his full cooperation. But for the present, Edward's support is sufficient."

"Mr. Abbott, I would like to hear your thoughts. Do you have any additional information we should be including in this announcement? Any issues we should be aware of?"

Abbott, with a tightening of his jaw, got up and walked to the library windows. Closing the draperies on the outside world, he appeared to be all business, his nervousness was only evident by the slight sheen on his brow. Otherwise, Katherine thought he looked as if he were preparing to give a business briefing. *This man would keep it together. Maybe the interviews won't be as dreadful as I've feared.*

"You had better see this before we continue. I was sent the following disk in the mail along with the demand for $800,000 for the original." Looking over to his wife, regret etched on his face, Edward inserted the disk into the television and hit "play" before moving to the bar and pouring a double scotch.

Everyone in the library fell silent in anticipation, focused on the large screen mounted on the wall. Katherine hadn't been expecting to see actual evidence behind the blackmail. However, knowing the specifics would provide needed context. She made a mental note to ask Sally about her liability in participating in the cover up. Criminal acts were outside her field of expertise.

The island of light emanating from the monitor brought what looked to be a mid-priced hotel room into view, easily identified by the plastic card containing hotel rules mounted on the back of the door. A wide angle lens captured the entire 300 square foot space, empty except for a king size bed and the standard hotel-design furniture guaranteed to withstand years of harsh treatment. It was a tired room made all the more seamy by the small wattage bulbs in the ceiling fixture.

When the door of the room opened a few seconds later, the camera showed Edward Abbott entering the room with an Asian woman, young enough to be his daughter. The knife slim woman a full head shorter than Abbott, was shown supporting his taller, heavier frame, and with some difficulty she assisted him to walk on unsteady feet towards a rumpled unmade bed.

Dressed in a crisp turquoise silk cocktail dress, her long black hair and white skinned perfection were a sharp contrast to Abbott's rumpled appearance. While there was no sound on the video, Abbott seemed to be questioning the woman. The more unfazed she appeared, the more agitated he became. Then the screen went blank only to resume a couple of seconds later with Edward Abbott sprawled naked under the bed covers with the stunning girl's bare body wrapped securely in his arms. Composed like a picture of a happy couple after steamy sex, the girl's hair was spread over the pillow and tangled in the crook of Edward's arm. His relaxed expression gave the appearance of a man sexually spent.

When the monitor clicked off, Edward opened the drapes and looked first to his wife, then to Thomas and Katherine, all sitting in stunned silence. The video they had just watched had turned a cozy room into a clandestine chamber of secrets.

Katherine, still as stone, reviewed this bombshell. On one level, the film implied the two had engaged in an active romp in bed and were now asleep with the sheets carelessly gathered around their entwined bodies. A Hollywood director might have said, "Cut and print." On another level, she needed to know more about who and why this entire scene had been orchestrated.

"Not my finest hour," Edward remarked and sat off by himself on a club chair, his hands cradling a freshened drink.

There was just something in the video that didn't ring true. Katherine relied on her ability to read people. A brief experience in college theater had shown her how the set of someone's shoulders, the way they shifted their gaze, even the way they held their hands could signal if they were lying. Looking at this beaten man, Katherine decided that he had been tricked, the girl wasn't enticing Edward. She seemed emotionally uninvolved. Was she a professional? Someone who had participated in this kind of setup before? Edward wasn't pursuing her, she was leading him. If this had been an actual tryst where was the sexual tension? And what was in the missing footage?

"Mr. Abbott, do you remember anything about that evening?" Katherine's question was asked as delicately as she could manage. "Where you were earlier? Were you supposed to be meeting someone? Would there be any clues in your appointment diary?"

"I can't remember anything about that evening. My office appointment book is clear of meetings for the afternoon. In fact, I can't remember what I did earlier in that day."

Looking to Sweeney she asked, "Can we find someone to trace Mr. Abbott's whereabouts that day?"

"Yes. I know a private investigator I trust. I'll get in touch and get back to you. Aside from the obvious who and why, do you have anything you would like him to check out?"

"I would like to know why the blackmailer wanted $800,000, not more. How that amount of money was removed from the Foundation, and if we can return it secretly before the announcement is released?"

"I can take care of when the fiscal transfers took place and where they were sent. As for the missing funds, I am in the process of gathering the money together. Hopefully they can be returned before they are missed. Our investigator will have to find out how this video was taken," Sweeney said.

"Can he also find out if Mr. Abbott has any enemies, people who might have been hurt in a personal or business transaction?" Katherine added.

"Edward, I am going to ask you to meet with an investigator and see if he can turn up anything that connects you to either this video or the blackmailer. Not to worry, it's Sparkey. You know he'll be discrete." Sweeney said.

"I would like to know who this woman is and how she became involved in setting this trap," Megan interjected. "I'd like to talk to her, maybe get her to help us. That is only if it will help Edward," Megan added.

"Megan, you know Sparkey will get to the bottom of this scheme. He'll find out who and why. If it's a personal vendetta, or simply a crime of opportunity."

"All right, now down to our campaign." Sweeney's terse tone returned the group to the business at hand, after Megan's request reminded them of the personal element of this sordid affair. "Katherine, I would like you to prepare Edward for his upcoming interviews."

The air in the room immediately snapped to attention as if oxygen had been pumped into the library, infusing its inhabitants with energy.

"Mr. Abbott, have you reviewed the articles by the reporters I've identified to conduct your one-on-one interviews about your retirement? Is there anyone else you would rather speak with? Do you need any coaching in handling what will surely be difficult questions?"

"Your choices seem fine. I would like to have some sort of script to address any possible curve balls."

"Curve balls indeed," Katherine responded. "One might be the mention of your wife's relationship with Thomas Sweeney. How would you answer that without implying any nepotism?"

"Simply that I met her at a social function and suggested we have dinner. I wasn't aware of her relationship to Thomas, and even if I had been, I was smitten the moment she laughed at one of my poor jokes."

"And if the reporter digs for more?"

"I'm still smitten. I am one lucky fellow." A self-effacing Edward looked over to his wife with a sheepish smile.

"Good. Now, why is a young man of forty-two years-old retiring at the moment when Marathon Nutritionals is planning to expand and become a member of the stock exchange?"

"I strongly believe I am leaving the company at the perfect time for Gregory Pomeroy to assume control as chief financial officer. When a company embarks on its path towards membership on the NASDAQ, a lot of the preparation falls to the chief financial officer. It would be better for Gregory to be in place prior to Marathon going public."

"Now, Katherine, you see why Edward has been my trusted financial advisor for all these years," Sweeney remarked.

Nodding in agreement, she continued, "And how will you answer your early retirement? You are young to leave a career as stellar as yours."

"I have recently been diagnosed with hypertension." Surprised registered on Megan's face. "It's true, Love. But at this stage it's a warning to slow down."

Looking back to the group, he continued, "While I feel young, I am looking to reduce the hours and strain of my day-to-day responsibilities. I can only do that by retiring before my condition worsens, or I become truly ill. I want to step back and pursue my charitable endeavors." Looking at Megan, Edward's, face softened, "And, I want to spend more time with my wife. She has given up her career and entirely too much in support of my goals."

Katherine had a moment of jealousy watching Megan and Edward share a private glance. There was no question they deeply loved one another. Would she ever find a life's partner with the same devotion?

"Mr. Sweeney, I believe Mr. Abbott can handle himself in his interviews. And, I will be there to redirect any questions that go beyond the issues we just reviewed. With the details in the release and Mr. Abbott's publicly available record, we should be able to keep this crisis under wraps. The changing of officers is a solid and clean announcement. It shouldn't cause unexpected inquiries."

"Are you sure, Katherine?" Mrs. Abbott asked in a tone that implied she wasn't.

"You have my promise to do my very best. We don't really have any other choice. By granting interviews we are implying that Marathon has nothing to hide. You know there is never a one hundred percent guarantee that our planning will prevent problematic leaks."

Watching Sweeney stand, Katherine took the hint that the meeting was over. She walked to where Edward sat and offered her hand. "Mr. Abbott, I know you don't like speaking to the media. I truly understand and thank you for agreeing to our plan." Offering her hand to Mrs. Abbott, she nodded. "I'll do my very best to protect your husband from potentially harmful questions."

Standing and accepting her outstretched hand, Abbott looked resigned. "I will do my best not to disappoint you. I can't believe how I could have been so stupid."

6

The phone's shrill ring jolted Sandra from a blissful sleep. She had been curled up next to Ian, oblivious of the world outside her bungalow. She lifted the receiver and heard the voice of her secretary, Alice, the only one who knew how to reach her. Moving as far away from the slumbering Ian as the phone cord allowed, Sandra steeled herself for what had to be bad news. Alice knew not to bother her when she was out of town, especially when on vacation.

"Ms. Charney, I think you should know that something is going on at the office."

"Alice, can you be a bit more specific? Cut to the chase."

"Well, I spotted Ms. Cunningham getting out of the executive elevator. I've never seen her even near it before...Ms. Charney, are you still there?"

As she considered Alice's information, Sandra seethed. With a soft "OK," she hung up to consider her next moves. Something was going on with Ms. cheerful bit-of-fluff, Katherine Cunningham. If Cunningham hadn't been with the firm for as long as she had, she'd fire her ass for insubordination, even if there was nothing to pin it on. Now, in this politically correct society, she'd be accused of discriminating against a younger woman. Shit! Sensing that her carefully controlled career was in jeopardy by this over-credentialed upstart, Sandra's instincts demanded she find out what was going on.

After a highly gratifying evening together, both she and Ian had fallen into an exhausted sleep. Already angered by the call, she was now pissed that it had awakened Ian. So be it. Looking towards her bed mate struggling to open his eyes, she cussed the day she ever met miss perfect Cunningham. From the first Sandra had kept the girl on a short leash. She was an excellent researcher and writer. Yet, there was something about her Sandra found threatening to her status, position and authority at Marathon.

"Sorry darling. Have to check something out. I'll be back shortly." She walked to his side of the bed and, gave Ian a deep kiss. "Hold that thought." Opening the closet, Sandra pulled out a simple shift and thongs. Dressed, her mind in battle mode, she quietly closed the door behind her.

Sandra approached the registration desk upon reaching the lobby. "Miss? Where is your business center?" Given directions and the assurance that it was open, Sandra headed to the office in search of a phone. She couldn't use her cell, because in her rush to leave New York, she had forgotten to add international calling to her plan. In all her years with the company, Alice had only called her once when she was on vacation and that was to tell her that her mother had died.

Entering the business office, Sandra checked in with the receptionist who said she would connect her to the international operator. She settled into a small booth and placed a long distance call to her secretary. Alice would be at her desk awaiting her call.

"Alice, was Ms. Cunningham with anyone?"

"No. And she went straight to her office."

"Well then, I need you to do something for me. Can you get into her office now?"

"Yes, it's a little after 6 pm here. There shouldn't be any problem. I'll just have to wait for her to leave."

"Good. I want you to look for anything unusual. Be careful not to disturb any papers. Check her computer and her inbox and call me. I'm sixteen hours ahead. But don't worry, just have the hotel page me and I'll return your call."

After hanging up, Sandra headed for the small bar off to one side of the lobby. She needed to think. Signaling to the waiter, she ordered a brandy and sat at a table, crossing her slim legs while focused on this latest challenge to her authority. With her mind puzzling over Alice's call, she was unaware of her top leg pumping in beat with her racing heart. Alice was someone who could sniff trouble before it created difficulties for Sandra. If her secretary thought something was going on behind her back, there was a ninety-nine percent chance there was.

Unaware that she had chewed one of her fingernails clean of its polish, Sandra sipped her brandy and continued stewing. Never to her knowledge had Cunningham defied one of her directives. Not once in seven years. Patience wasn't Sandra's strength, but thirty years of experience told her to wait. She needed more information.

7

At first glance, Marathon Nutritionals' research laboratory located in the wilds of New Jersey appeared not to have changed in more than 200 years. When Thomas Sweeney moved the company from Iowa to New York, he bought the 18th century brick factory and built a state-of-the-art scientific laboratory within its aged walls. The idea was to camouflage the company's forward looking research with under-the-radar trappings.

Dr. Shen Lu, director of Marathon's research, was given a free hand and liberal budget to build a facility that would create nutraceuticals, products that provide health and medical benefits, to a large audience of consumers. Those wedded to traditional pharmaceutical-grade drugs for treatment of various illnesses and conditions might call Dr. Lu's research junk science. However, in its twenty year history, the company had proven naysayers wrong by becoming the country's number one source of nutritional supplements. The company's success proved Sweeney's prediction that there would be a growing health conscious public seeking alternative therapies.

The photo on Dr. Shen Lu's desk pictured a smiling Thomas Sweeney and Shen Lu in army uniforms. It had been taken almost forty years ago in front of a field hospital in Vietnam. The two men, one tall and thin, the other short and slight, became colleagues and friends during four war-torn years spent at this medical outpost. Whenever Shen looked at the photo he thought of just how far the two men had come. Shen had been the chief medical officer and First Lieutenant Thomas Sweeney, had been in charge of staffing and operations.

He thought of their first meeting, wondering how one year of medical school with a degree in chemistry would be of any help in suturing, amputating and treating all manner of physical horrors. "Listen, doc," Sweeney said, quietly responding to Shen's initial doubts. "I can get and organize anything you need. Just tell me what you want."

Shen remembered looking at the quietly confident young man, about the same age, and knew he would be able to count on him as a steady, second in command.

"Irrigate that wound while I clamp the bleed," instructed Shen not twenty-four hours after Sweeney's arrival. Watching to make sure the equipment had gone from the sterilizer to the operating table without being contaminated, reassured Shen of the man's seriousness of purpose. A surprise was the young man's facility for handling medical emergencies.

"Now, hand me the instruments, handle first, as I ask for them." Shortly after his initial surgery Shen began relying on Thomas to pitch in when the medical team was short staffed. Working alongside Shen to clean, patch, and stitch the wounded, they had bonded into what had become a life-long friendship.

"Mail call." shouted the soldier as he handed Shen a thick envelope from home. "Thomas, here's the latest AMA Journal. Let me know when you have time and I'll leave it for you."

"OK, but I'd rather have a drink and drill you about your great grandfather's apothecary."

"Why? This is the 20th Century," Shen had responded, a bit surprised the first time Thomas had raised the subject. It was a topic dear to his heart and one he had been fascinated with ever since he was a young boy and had found notes about his great grandfather's practice in Peking, China.

"Because, when and if I get out of this morass of human suffering I'm going to start a company to manufacture nutritional products. As an amateur athlete, I have been using protein supplements for years. I believe there are natural substances to help people maintain good health and strong bodies. If I'm right these substances will enable many to ward off onset of serious illnesses."

During late evening hours recovering after a day of physical and mental exhaustion from treating the raw flesh traumatized by war, Thomas pried Shen with questions relating to oriental medicine.

"You may be on to something, my friend," Shen responded. "The whole theory of traditional Chinese medicine is to keep the body's organs working at their optimum. When an organ or other system is out of balance, the body exhibits certain symptoms. The apothecary would, after an examination of pulse, breath, shape of the tongue, and other physical indicators of illness, compound formulas designed to restore that balance. When I get out of this nightmare I plan to study my great grandfather's notes and see if I can develop modern day equivalents."

"Oriental formulas?" Thomas asked. "Shen, would you loan me a copy to study?"

Laughing at his weary friend, Shen replied, "Only if you can read Mandarin. I have been studying the language for years and I still have trouble deciphering the old master's notes."

Shen's post-medical school studies on natural herbal derivatives as cures, not merely palliative substances, was a lifelong passion. His great grandfather would have understood. As a 19th Century apothecary, he was known for the consistency of his treatments. But there had been no formal studies to verify his ancestor's achievements. Shen was investigating the old man's diaries that included anecdotal results, in hope of recreating his formulas. This was no easy task. As an American born child of second generation Chinese American parents, he first had to become proficient in Mandarin Chinese, then in deciphering his great grandfather's scientific notations.

It was six-thirty Tuesday evening, and Shen Lu was the only one left in the lab. Seated on an ergonomically designed chair, he was in the process of finalizing a report he was certain would make Thomas smile. When Thomas had set out to open Marathon Nutritionals he invited his friend to join as a co-founder. But Shen reneged. He wanted to remain a pure scientist. Management wasn't his field. The result was Shen became Thomas Sweeney's unofficial partner, sharing in patents and profits. A fact known to very few. Not only were the men colleagues, together they had built a company based on their shared conviction that people could be treated with natural remedies.

While rereading his findings, Shen sat a bit straighter, proud of his latest research into cholesterol lowering substances. After months of testing he had successfully manufactured a pill of a naturally derived statin grown from red yeast rice. The miraculous substance had the capability of lowering high cholesterol, without the dangerously high concentrations found in pharmaceutically produced versions. His report was recommending that this latest discovery be moved to the top of the company's production schedule.

"Dr. Lu." The crisp voice announced the arrival of Victor Rosso, Marathon's chief operating officer and officially Shen's boss. A situation that was due entirely to the company's need for an official organization of its management. Shen unofficially reported only to Thomas Sweeney.

"May I have a few minutes?"

Turning to give the man his attention, he wondered what this bean counter wanted. To cut his budget? Question the purchase of a new piece of laboratory equipment? Or simply to bedevil him?

"I believe you intend to recommend the immediate production of a new herbal supplement, red yeast rice? I haven't seen any similar products being advertised. Why are you recommending we rush into production?"

"Victor, I am just finishing my production recommendations. Are you aware of the importance of this latest nutraceutical?"

Shen Lu looked at the bantam rooster of a man with suspicion born from years working under his authority. A man of small stature himself, there was something about the preening and posturing of Victor Rosso that disgusted him. He clearly was impressed with his own importance. Especially in assuming he had full authority over Shen and his department. A sham Shen encouraged to keep out of the little dictator's way.

"I am happy to review my recommendations with you Victor. I think you will see that with minimum changes to our production line, we can be on the market in six months. As for the timing, this will provide the necessary lead time to develop a marketing campaign and have the product stocked on store shelves."

As Victor Rosso strolled around the lab, running a hand over each of the recently installed pieces of polished chrome equipment, Shen knew the bean counter didn't know the importance of any of the advanced apparatus. Shen could see his calculating mind totaling their costs, unaware that the particular piece he had just dismissed had saved the company thousands of dollars and months in the development of what Shen believed to be the next miracle product.

Not wanting to have Victor go around him and hassle Thomas, Shen tried to explain the importance of rushing this new product into production. "Our research has verified the efficacy of a 5000-year-old substance for the 21st Century. Imagine how people suffering with high cholesterol will have a safe alternative to pharmaceutical drugs."

"We don't want to antagonize the FDA," Rosso declared as if speaking to an hourly employee. "Statins have long been an effective medical treatment for controlling that condition."

"Victor, we manufacture nutritional substances. Marathon's products are not classified as drugs and therefore outside the jurisdiction of the Food and Drug Administration."

Practiced at ignoring Victor's diatribes, Shen, while seeming to listen to a lecture on the dangers of inciting FDA disapproval, allowed his mind to drift to a recent conversation with Thomas about another hopeful avenue of research.

"Yes, Thomas. It looks as if initial testing of polyphenol is showing us another window into the body's cellular defense system."

"Shen, this could be huge. How far along are you in your research?"

"Polyphenol is the active ingredient found in green tea. We are testing to see if in concentrated forms it can unlink toxins from the body's cells before they become invasive and cause disease. If this proves to be correct, people will be able to take a concentrated form in a pill and enable their body's to flush harmful toxins out of their system naturally."

"Shen, where did you get the idea to look into green tea? People have been drinking it as an antioxidant for years. You just found an entirely new approach to unlocking its secrets."

"I got a clue on the properties of green tea from my great grandfather's journals. Thomas there is so much to explore in those texts. Sometimes, when a glimmer of something jumps off the page, I think he is looking over my shoulder."

Abruptly brought back to the present by Victor's confrontational lecture about disrupting his manufacturing schedule, Shen politely interrupted. Whenever Victor went off on a power trip, Shen found he could mollify the man by his quiet acceptance. Anything to get the odious man to leave him alone. "Victor, the report isn't ready. I will have it on your desk as soon as it is completed."

"Well, when I see the costs associated with changing our operations, I'll consider your suggestion that we rush this new item into production." Nodding to Shen, Rosso left the laboratory as suddenly as he had appeared.

Returning to his report, Shen thought, how can I let this imbecile decide the validity of our newest discovery? Shen's father would have had voiced one of his favorite Chinese proverbs. *There's no need to speak out what everybody knows.* "Sorry Dad, I prefer Sun Tzu's - He who knows when he can fight and when he cannot will be victorious."

*   *   *

Rubbing his hands in satisfaction, Victor Rosso returned to his office located at the opposite side of the building. His impromptu visit to the laboratory had the desired effect of putting the good doctor on notice that he, not Shen Lu, decided what and when a product was manufactured. Yes, the little chemist would do as Victor instructed. After all, his entire laboratory budget was controlled by Victor.

Surveying his office as he settled in to find ways to hinder Dr. Lu's suggested change in the manufacturing schedule, Victor's eyes fell on plaques attesting to his CPA accreditation and Outstanding Business Leader Citation awarded by the local Chamber of Commerce. Each achievement won after years of financial struggle in one menial accounting job after another. Finally, he was secure having spent almost a decade helping Thomas Sweeney build a profitable company.

Yes, he would delay the introduction of Dr. Lu's latest product and schedule it for the following quarter. That would keep the annoying oriental in line. The costs of his equipment demands were getting out of control.

When Sweeney saw the financial results of changes he had been making in operations, he would have to recognize Victor's contributions to the company's bottom line. By year-end Victor expected no less than a 15% bonus for his hard work.

8

Thomas Sweeney sat in his library reviewing the evening's meeting with a sense that all were on board, committed to his plan for announcing Edward's retirement. Katherine would keep the questions coming to make sure all i's were dotted, and t's crossed. Edward would, with Megan's assistance, try to find clues to identify the blackmailer. Was it someone he knew? Someone he crossed? Or simply someone in need of that amount of money and Edward was an easy target?

Thomas had to find the blackmailer, return the $800,000 unnoticed, and find the woman in the video. Reaching for his phone, he punched in the number of a childhood friend, John Sparks. While Thomas had gone to medical school and into the army, John, Sparkey to his friends, had apprenticed with his father, a private investigator working for a select group of corporate clients.

As kids, they would play a game of solving crimes in which one or the other would be the murderer, thief, or blackmailer. Their training manuals were the mysteries of Sir Arthur Conan Doyle, P.D. James and Agatha Christie who generously shared the methods of criminals and detectives with their readers. Sherlock Holmes was one of Thomas's favorite detectives. Sparkey's was Hercule Poirot.

"Sparkey, how are you old man?"

"Thomas, you're my age. What do you mean old man?"

Ignoring the usual come-back, Thomas turned serious. "I know it's late, but could we meet tonight? There's something you can help me with and it's rather urgent."

"No, 'what have you been up to? How are the wife and kiddies?' It must be urgent! Of course I'll lend a hand. Is your place in half an hour soon enough?"

"That would be fine. I'll pour the single malt to assist those little grey cells Poirot is always talking about."

Sweeney hung up but couldn't help thinking he was beginning a clandestine event with the potential to ruin not only himself, but the entire company. Not for the first time since his wife had passed away almost twenty years before did he yearn for her sage advice. Lucy understood the ramifications of his corporate responsibilities and had an unerring way of clarifying his thoughts. He could hear her soft voice, "Darling, you skipped over the most important element in your plan. Regroup. Here, I'll write it down as a reminder." Oh how he missed her still.

*   *   *

Greeting Sparkey exactly one half hour later, Sweeny took the man's leather jacket. "Married life agrees. Not only are you on time, you've lost at least twenty pounds since we last got together."

"The best partnership I could ever have imagined. You should try it before you get any older."

"Been there. And, I loved every minute of my life with Lucy. It was just too short. One year you get married, and two entirely short years later God changes his mind and says you've had enough happiness for your lifetime. By now, I've adjusted."

"I always thought you and Lucy were a charmed couple. She was your perfect complement…an optimist to bring you out of your overly-serious self."

"I wished I had been stricken with cancer. She wasn't meant to suffer. Sparkey I couldn't save her. All my research didn't help. Her death still drives me." Thomas felt his friend's hand gently squeeze his shoulder. It reminded him that Sparkey had been there for his entire marriage and stood by him throughout Lucy's illness.

"Urgent? Single Malt? I seem to remember hints that I may be of assistance." Sparkey's upbeat tone snapped Thomas back to the present.

"I am a man of my word." Pouring two drinks and adding two cubes each, Thomas handed Sparkey one glass and took a sip from his own. "First, I would like to show you a video." Dimming the lights, they sat back to view the eight minute show. Thomas knew Sparkey had met Edward Abbott several times, first at his wedding to Megan and later during gatherings of both families.

"Thomas I like Edward. How is the scene in the video even possible? Abbott defines the term straight arrow."

"This was sent to Edward along with a demand of $800,000, or the information would be made public."

"How are you handling this as far as Marathon is concerned?"

"We are in the process of announcing Edward's retirement and the appointment of Gregory Pomeroy to the position of CFO. But I need to replace the funds quietly and find the bastard who set this into motion. I don't believe Edward Abbott has an enemy in the world. My guess is it's someone who knows he can access that odd amount of money. There is also the possibility that someone wants to blacken the Company's reputation. Make it unlikely that we could raise money for expansion by becoming a public company."

"Can I see that video?"

Removing the disk from the monitor, Thomas handed it to his friend. "Can you determine who or how this was shot?"

"I have a friend who knows people you shouldn't. However, he may be of some help. Let me borrow this. Do you happen to have the mailing envelope?"

"Right here." Sweeney handed Sparkey the paper sleeve along with the simple mailing envelope. Sparkey gave both a quick look before placing the disk into its wrapper and inserting it into the padded envelope.

"The address is printed in black ball point ink, but the manila mailer has no post mark or return address to assist in tracking the package back to its sender. Maybe the DVD has something on it to help track down the videographer." Sparkey said.

"Edward told me it had been left with his doorman Sunday evening. The doorman was new and his description could match any bike messenger in the city."

"I am assuming that both the sleeve and mailer have been handled by multiple hands?"

"Yes. I didn't think about fingerprints. Sorry."

"I'll check and get back to you by tomorrow. What bothers me is the missing footage between the time Edward enters the room and the time he is shown in bed with that Asian beauty."

"I wondered about that as well. Time to set the stage?" Sweeney was anxious but hopeful that Sparkey would find a lead. "Obviously this is all hush hush."

Nodding his agreement, Sparkey stood, finished the last of his drink and handing his glass to Thomas, swore, "Right buddy. Not to worry. You have my word to work like a shadow. We'll nail this guy."

*   *   *

It had been awhile since his last case of skullduggery. Rubbing his hands together, Sparkey's mind was already exploring the rationale of blackmailers…those who used fear for profit…and reminding himself that those profits weren't always financial.

Sparkey exited Thomas's brownstone and hailed a taxi. He gave the driver an address for a bar in alphabet city. Resurrection was frequented by old time Polish immigrants who had settled in the area during and after World War II. In the constantly evolving Manhattan, this was one neighborhood that had so far evaded gentrification.

"Hi Theo. A draft." As Sparkey settled on a stool he noticed that the bar was only half full. "Slow night?"

"Yea. If it doesn't pick up by midnight, I'm going to close up."

"You need a new crowd. Your usual's look like they're from the previous century. What are you going to do when they die out?"

"Any ideas how I should go about that?" Theo asked.

"Why not see if you can get some of the college crowd? There must be a few living in these old buildings. It's probably one of the last affordable areas in New York."

Nodding, Theo resumed washing glasses, a job he'd been doing when Sparkey arrived. "How?"

"Post a sign in the window offering ladies free wine and beer, Thursday's from 4-6."

"I could do that. Henry over there, works in the NYU bookstore. He could spread the word." Smiling, Theo stopped washing and walked up to this longtime customer and looked him squarely in the eye. "Now, what can I do for you?"

Putting down his beer, Sparkey returned the smile. "I wonder if you can direct me to someone who might do some secret filming."

"If you mean hidden cameras and such, that's illegal."

Sparkey often hired Theo or one of his sons to follow a suspect. While he never asked to have someone filmed, he knew that there were people in the old man's circle who would.

"This is personal. I need to find a blackmailer. Anything you can do will be appreciated."

Theo nodded. "I may know of someone who on occasion will do a job like that. Here," and scribbling a name and address on a napkin handed it to Sparkey. "He should be home now. I'll call ahead."

"Thanks. I'll see if I can get some kids to stop by and bring their friends." Waving the napkin, Sparkey got up and placed a twenty dollar bill on the bar. He hoped Theo's contact would be able to help identify the person who had filmed the devastating little movie.

9

Walking five short blocks to the address Theo had given him, Sparkey, stopped in front of a brick row house and headed for a side entrance. After ringing the bell, he was soon confronted by a young man dressed in badly worn jeans and t-shirt with *Don't fuck with me. That's my job!* printed across his boney chest. Sparkey sniffed the air and noted the distinctive smell of weed. The young man's eyes, however, were clear. Drugs, even recreational ones, were never Sparkey's thing. But in his line of work, he knew when a person was high or simply mellow.

"Jake Conner?" Watching for some reaction and not getting any, he continued. "Theo said you might be able to help me." Not waiting for an invitation, Sparkey sidestepped around the hostile young man blocking the doorway and handed over an envelope. "I need to know how and who made this video. And, I need it yesterday."

"Yeah?"

"Yes, Mr. Connor. Will you at least watch this video and tell me what you think?"

Opening the envelope and removing a disk, Jake Connor shook his head and he jabbed a forefinger into Sharkey's chest. "How did you get this, pal?"

The hostility of the tall scraggly youth surprised Sparkey. Needing a minute to regroup, he looked around the apartment. He was surprised to see an open floor-through space with a back garden area just visible at the far end of the room. If this same apartment were located any place else in Manhattan even Sparkey with a healthy income, wouldn't have been able to afford it. *Well, well an entrepreneur*, he thought.

"Look...may I call you Jake?"

Given more of his hostile attitude, Sparkey lowered his voice and softened his edginess. "I understand why you might not want to help me with an obviously illegally taken film, but I promise you that I am not here to cause trouble. That video is, however, causing some very nice people major problems. Will you please help me?"

Jake waved the disk in Sparkey's face and snapped, "This little item isn't a gift." Waiting a few seconds, Jake finally, reluctantly, closed the apartment door.

"Business must be good, Mr. Connor. You have every artistic New Yorker's dream...a full floor-through apartment and garden."

"How did you get this, man? I need to know. Don't tell me its privileged info." Jake's hostility had lessened to a simmer as he led his visitor to his office and slumped into his desk chair.

Sparkey radar signaled pay dirt. "It's yours!"

"Yup. And I am not proud of it."

"We had better sit and figure this out. My client, who is also my oldest friend, needs to find the source quickly and quietly."

Inserting the DVD in his computer, Jake watched the edited version. "Look man, I was told to edit the original. I got my instructions via phone. So I don't see how I can help you."

Sparkey had to know how Jake had become involved in a blackmailer's web. Years of watching people for lies led him to believe that while the kid would walk on the edges of legality, in truth he probably wasn't a criminal. But this little set-up was.

"Look, what do I call you?"

"My name is John Sparks. Sparkey to my friends. OK?" Trying not to rush the reluctant Jake Conner, he said, "So how did you get involved in this?"

Jake began to fidget. "I was dumb. Went for the money."

Sitting back and waiting for Jake to settle, Sparkey thought, *Shit! Now I'm not only responsible for fixing Thomas's problems, but making sure Jake doesn't get into trouble. Blackmail isn't the crime of a well-mannered citizen.*

*   *   *

In the fifteen minutes since arriving, Sparkey hadn't been able to get Jake to talk, other than to tell him he was a film student and took surveillance jobs to pay his tuition.

He just paced back and forth in the area equipped with monitors, editing equipment, and other paraphernalia he used for both his university projects and more profitably, for his side business, surveillance. Then, slowly, the kid began to respond to basic questions. The conversation in the cluttered low-lit apartment had the two stepping around each other like fighters sizing one another up before throwing that first punch.

"So Pauley introduced you to someone who gave you a phone number? Don't you make it a rule to meet each of your clients?" Sparkey asked.

"My first mistake," Jake replied. "My next was to trust this twerp who couldn't follow an elephant walking down Fifth Avenue."

"A university chum?"

"I thought so. Anyway, the job intrigued me. I was to call this number and if I liked the assignment, I'd earn $5000 for four hours of work."

"That's a handsome fee for four hours. And…"

"And, an obviously disguised voice told me that there was a hotel room waiting for me to install my equipment. All I had to do was setup the camera focused on the adjoining room. Then wait a couple of hours, collect the footage, pack up and leave." Jake faced Sparkey with a look of agitation that bore out his plight. "I had no way of knowing that I'd have to drill a hole in the wall for the lens, or what I was going to film. I swear!"

"When you found out couldn't you back out?"

"No, damn it! If I'd been thinking clearly, simply the amount of money for the job should have screamed at me: Don't even consider taking this assignment."

"Look, I'm starved." Picking up his cell phone Jake called out for a pepperoni pizza with extra cheese. "Want a brew? I'm going to have another before we dig your client and me out of this shit!"

Not waiting for Sparkey to answer, Jake headed over to the galley kitchen. Opening the under-the-counter refrigerator, he pulled out two bottles of Blue Moon, flipped off the caps and handing one to Sparkey, chugged down half of his. "Let's take a break and wait for the pie. OK? I need to think on this."

Nodding, Sparkey took a sip of his beer. Seated in an adjacent desk chair, he turned away so he wasn't looking directly at the kid and hoped it would allow him to regain his composure. It was all Sparkey could do not to scream in frustration. Here he was sitting with the photographer, and the kid just didn't get the urgency of finding the man who hired him to film this dirty little video.

Answering the doorbell, Jake handed the delivery boy a twenty dollar bill. "Keep the change, it's on him." Closing the door, Jake held out his hand.

"I guess I could eat a slice," Jake said putting a twenty on top of the warm box.

"You know, Jake, whatever this assignment is all about I'm on your side." Swiveling his chair to catch the kid's reaction, he was pleased to see him nodding back. "So, let me give you some background while we eat. It will help me decide where we go from here. With your help I can find the blackmailer and no one will ever connect you to this scheme."

Sparkey told Jake about the man in the video. "To get a copy of the original disk, the man had embezzled $800,000 from my client's charitable foundation to pay off the blackmailer. Jake, I know this man. We've played cards together. I was at his wedding. I'm telling you, he's as straight as they come. Smart, a loving husband, and relative of my client by marriage. Hell this guy is so upright, his shorts are ironed."

"I figured. He didn't look like a creep. But I couldn't back out even after I saw what was going on in that hotel room. I couldn't help him. And those thugs weren't anyone I wanted to challenge. Whoever this creep is, he made me a criminal."

"Thugs? What thugs?" Sparkey all but yelled.

"The two thugs who set up this guy on that little film."

Sipping on his beer, Sparkey stepped back, giving the kid some space and silently watched him scarf down the last slice of pizza.

"Look, the man in the video is Edward Abbott, and he was the CFO of Marathon Nutritionals. The founder of the company is my childhood friend, Thomas Sweeney. This is personal. In addition to Abbott and Sweeney, you have to be protected. Now we have proof that Abbott was set up, I must find out who and why. Jake, I need your help to make this go away. I need to do it yesterday!"

*   *   *

With the remains of the pizza joining empty beer bottles on the floor, Jake broke the silence. "Man, blackmail isn't my bag. And this whole deal was suspect from the first. I have never drilled a hole in the wall of a hotel to film another room. I don't film sex romps. You've got to believe me."

"I believe you. Theo knew I wouldn't work with you if he hadn't assured me you could be trusted."

Just knowing that enabled Jake to refocus and think about protecting himself. "OK. Since this client was a weirdo, and that edited video isn't my style, I'll help you track down the players. But, you've got to promise to keep my name out of this. This whole gig was illegal. I can't go to jail for my stupidity."

Sparkey looked at the 25-year old and realized that Jake was more than his skill in surveillance. Regardless of his sloppy lifestyle, street lingo, and anti-adult prejudices, Jake was saying he'd use his skills to help, but Sparkey had better not screw him.

"Jake, did he threaten you?" Sparkey hoped this scheme, whatever it entailed, was orchestrated for profit not vengeance. If Jake had been threatened, this was indeed a dangerous situation.

"Not directly. But it was creepy. Yes, I tape people. I usually tail someone to a restaurant, apartment building, or public space and film whoever they meet. A man following his wife or, a wife following her husband. Sometimes it's just a meeting where my client wants to identify the players. It's a profitable business and to my mind it's okay. This is sick. It's not OK."

With a nod Jake indicated for Sparkey to join him at the back of the apartment, an area that looked like a kid's play room. The supposed living room area of the cluttered floor-through apartment was set up with a large monitor and a table holding assorted gaming consoles and hand-held remotes. Along with a sofa and club chairs, this was apparently where Jake decompressed from hours spent at his editing chores. "We might as well be comfortable, while we take a look at the original footage."

"You have the original film?" Sparkey whispered, feeling like someone had given him a present. "Let's see if we can find some clue to identifying the blackmailer, or the girl."

"I only know the client is a he because some of my instructions came by phone. As for the footage, I kept the original because I didn't trust the guy. Now I'm glad I didn't film over it."

Going to his desk and reaching underneath for a locked cabinet, Jake spun the combination and opening the metal door, withdrew a plastic box encased DVD. Slamming the cabinet closed, he returned to Sparkey sitting on the edge of a chair in wait. Jake pushed a variety of remotes off to one side of the table, and inserted the DVD into the monitor and let it run.

Sparkey fixed his eyes on the unfolding scene. The film opened to show the hidden camera being positioned at a hole in the common wall between two rooms. He guessed Jake wanted a record of his setup and positioning the camera would be a crucial bit of information if the assignment went sour.

As the film continued, the lens narrowed its focus and Sparkey saw the adjacent hotel room, along with the soundless images he had already seen...the sight of Abbott entering the room, walking with the help of the exotic young woman with long stick straight black hair and white skin. Abbott seemed intent on wanting the attractive woman to answer his questions. His hair no longer in place as he became more and more agitated at the woman who remained calm, not even a wrinkle to mar her perfect brow. She simply stood a short distance away unfazed by his torrent of words.

Then the missing footage that concerned Sparkey from the beginning came into view. Licking his dry lip Sparkey saw Abbott place his hands on the girl's shoulders to stop her in mid stride. Seeming to understand, the woman gently removed his hands, and turning towards the camera, picked up a phone and made a call. Was it room service? What was going on? Abbott was still riled up, but waited for her to hang up.

Turning away from Abbott, the girl walked towards the door. Was she leaving? But then she open the door to admit two rough-looking bruisers. As he watched the girl, he saw one of the thugs walk to Abbott and jam a needle into his arm. Abbott slumped against the large man, who picked him up as if his 190 pounds was inconsequential, and stretched him out on the bed. He then stripped him bare and began shouting something at the cowering girl. Focused on Abbott, the girl was unaware of the second man walking up behind her. Quick as a snake he inserted a syringe into her arm just above her elbow, and she instantly collapsed against him. When the man had her stripped out of her clothes, he placed the limp body on the bed next to Abbott, both breasts clearly visible, and positioned her head in the crook of his arm. Abbott, out cold, and naked from the neck to his hips, looked relaxed, a side effect of the injection. The girl, posed as she was, appeared to be sleeping, cuddled in the arms of her lover. Taking a final look at their work, the two bruisers left the room.

"Jake, can you replay the part with the thugs? There has to be some telltale sign in their build, walk, or dress."

Shaking his head, Sparkey couldn't for the moment figure out what was bothering him about the two men. "Did you see anything that would give us any clues Jake?"

"Nope. But I remember I was shaking so hard I couldn't use my cell phone. When I had finished filming, I was supposed to call the guy for further instructions. I remember saying, 'Something's come up. I have to pack up. Where do you want the tape?' And the gravelly voice on the other end of the phone gave me an address in the Bronx with instructions to leave the recording with a woman who answered the door. She would give me an envelope containing my fee."

"But you said you got additional instructions to edit the footage? When did that happen?"

"When I got to this address a Spanish-looking older woman encased in tight black jeans and a glittered up t-shirt handed me an envelope. 'Senor, para usted,' she said."

I wanted to question her but she just shook her head and closed the door to the building. I was too stressed to even open it to see if he had paid the full amount. I'm usually careful to make sure my expenses had been included. In this case the expenses included the hotel room and taxis to carry all of my equipment to and from the hotel. But when I got home and opened the envelope, it contained a note telling me that the disk would be delivered later that evening and I would receive a call telling me how he wanted it edited. My fee hadn't been included. The bastard! He knew I wouldn't edit the disk if I'd been paid."

Walking back to the kitchen for another beer, Jake declared, "I want this to go away. Maybe together we could find the culprit and shut him down. Hell, I want my life back. I should have forgotten the money and refused to edit the video. Should' a, would 'a, could 'a, doesn't help me now."

Returning, he saw Sparkey, shoulders slumped, but with a jaw tightened in determination. "When I had packed up and got ready to leave the room I decided I needed some insurance." Seeing the man's eyes spark with interest, Jake continued, "So, when I got to the lobby, I headed over to the reception desk. Boy was I relieved to find that the clerk was a young co-ed. While she was busy on the computer, I turned the hotel's registry around and checked the listing of the day's guests. Unfortunately, I found the name of my company, JR film productions listed. The one name not even remotely similar to the Thomas's, Smiths and Jones on the register was that of an Asian female, but no mention of her visitor. I wrote her name down on a slip of paper and placed it in the disk holder." Removing a slip of lined note paper, Jake handed it over to Sparkey. "It's probably not her real name. Let me find out if she was a hotel regular. We don't want to alert anyone to our snooping."

As Sparkey rubbed the back of his neck, a sign of concentration that he'd had since grade school, he knew he had to have a plan, an air tight approach, before he and Jake went any further. "Jake, I have a bad feeling about this. Those thugs are Asian. They just follow orders. Even if we found them and they spoke English, they wouldn't talk."

With the monitor off, the room was silent. Sparkey had felt the terror from the unseen hand that had set this trap in motion. Yes he would track back and most certainly identify the blackmailer. But in his experience, this wasn't about money. Money may be the currency, but the fear he felt after viewing the original video meant that this plot to discredit Abbott was personal.

"Now you know the situation," Jake said. "Where do you want to go from here?"

"I hope you got the full $5000."

"Yeah. In cash." Jake rose, took both disks and just stood there. "Sparkey, there are people I can question that you can't. I'll start with the girl and get back to you."

"Good idea. Can you print me individual photos of the girl and each of the thugs? I have a couple of people who might give us some idea of who they are. I've worked with them before and know they won't tip our hand."

"Yup. It'll take a couple of minutes. Do you want another brew while I make those prints?"

"Nope, I'm full." As Jake went back to his desk, Sparkey opened his cell and called Thomas. "Sorry to bother you, but didn't you say that you had a gal involved in the Marathon part of this operation? What I want to know is she smart, good looking, and would she help me track down some information?"

"Yes to each of your questions. As for her willingness, I don't want her involved in anything illegal. If you can promise her safety, then I will ask her first thing tomorrow. Give me an address and time to meet you. I think she will agree to at least hear you out."

Closing his phone, Sparkey waited for Jake and the photos. Tomorrow would be a long day. Time was ticking. The announcement was to be released in less than three days. To make this go away, he'd have to have things wrapped up by then.

10

Katherine arrived home a little after 10 pm and headed for the wine rack. Pouring a glass of Malbec, she reviewed the evening's revelations, especially Edward Abbott's reaction to the video. The good news was he'd been willing to accept her guidance, understanding the role he'd be playing for reporters. But from the moment the blackmailer's film finished playing to the stunned group, he had deflated. She'd have to find a way to transform Edward back into the executive leader. There couldn't be even a hint that there was anything other than his retirement behind their announcement.

This isn't just an assignment. It's corporate executive versus a criminal. And, I'm part of the defense team.

Kicking off her heels as she headed into her bedroom, she shed clothes faster than changing channels on her TV. Wrapped in her terry robe, Katherine reached for the phone.

"Sally? Am I interrupting anything important?"

"You mean am I entertaining? Nope. What's up?"

"Am I legally in trouble if I participate in a cover-up?"

"Say that again?"

"I need to know if I am privy to certain information, but not actually involved in anything criminal, if I could be in trouble?"

"And you can't divulge the specifics?"

"Right!"

"You haven't assisted in any criminal act?"

"No."

"You are simply there to do damage control with the media?"

"At this point, that's the picture. On the one hand it's all straight forward PR stuff. Something Sandra would usually handle."

"Sandra's turf? And you're on it? Now that is interesting. Hell with the law, I'd better hire a private security detail for you. When the Bitch returns she'll be merciless."

"Sally. Enough. Sandra can wait. Am I in trouble legally if I only tell part of the story?"

"Your exposure to certain information would classify you as a possible witness. As long as you don't lie under oath, you're safe. Just remember, if you are asked to aid a criminal act, or even a dicey one, you call me before saying or promising anything."

"But, Sally, when I prepare my news release I will be tailoring the information. I won't be twisting the truth or being dishonest, just communicating only part of the story."

"So what else is new? Isn't that what your profession is always accused of? Spinning the truth?"

"You know I don't see myself as a spin doctor. But in preparing corporate information, I have found that less is more. When I prepare a statement in a straight forward manner, there is less chance the media will get it wrong. Hell, I'm happy if they spell the name of the company's new product accurately!"

"Keep in mind that if things blow up, you will be implicated by association. So be extra careful of just how involved you become. Without specifics, I am afraid I can only remind you to be careful and call with any questions."

"Thanks. For now, I think I'm safe. I'll let you know if things change. Night."

Katherine felt a little more secure about her role and what it would entail. It was simply a matter of damage control. Deflecting interest away from Edward Abbott and towards the new CFO, George Pomeroy. If she had to brief Pomeroy, it would be to limit his answers to questions about his promotion. She didn't see a need to give him details surrounding Abbott's sudden retirement. If she was lucky Pomeroy wouldn't have to be involved.

As she sipped her wine, Katherine's thoughts turned to imagining how her situation would provoke Charncy into some Machiavellian act. She silently thanked Sweeney for planning to tell her boss he had requested Katherine's help in handling the announcement. But she knew that the older woman couldn't treat her normally. What had she ever done to cause her ire?

One time she had sent a draft for a speech to Sandra for approval. Only minutes had passed when her phone rang. "Cunningham, where did this quote from the VP of Human Resources come from? You are never to speak to anyone in senior management." Katherine could by now gauge her boss's level of anger by the frost in her voice. She could freeze a martini when sufficiently enraged.

"Sandra, the quote came from an announcement sent to our department last week. I simply thought it was a good fit with Mr. Brown's speech." She could still hear her boss's response. It was total silence, leaving Katherine staring at a dead phone.

In seven years Katherine had yet to figure out why in a department of six she was the only one to incur Sandra's enmity. True she was the only female, the four other members of the communications department were men, all with journalism backgrounds. One had a Dad with *The New York Times* and was raised to follow in his footsteps. Marathon was his first step on that career path. The other men ranged in age from 25 to 55 and seemed to work well with Charney. It was a small department so if even one of the men had incurred Charney's wrath, everyone would have heard about it. She had learned early on in her career not to deviate from Charney's dictates. Finding her responsibilities to be eminently satisfying, Katherine was usually left alone to prepare the research or written materials her boss required. In spite of keeping out of her boss's line of fire, the only positive comments to the quality of her work was her latest promotion to vice president of the department. Heaven forbid she'd receive an actual compliment. Well, she was getting tired of the tension and wondered if Sandra Charney was jealous of her having graduated Magna Cum Laude with her Masters from Columbia. Or, was the ice maiden really that insecure about working with a younger woman?

Returning to the task at hand, Katherine had to make sure all requests for interviews resulting from the Abbott announcement were directed to her. *How was the question?* It seemed that the entire press corps knew if they wanted to speak to any executive at Marathon, they had to go through Charney. This was the system reporters had followed for more than a decade. Those who tried to work around Charney, were placed on a black list never to be admitted to Marathon's offices or given the opportunity to speak to any of the company's employees.

Standing straighter, Katherine smiled, knowing that she would finally be working directly with three top reporters. *I'm sure they will be very interested in what I have to say.* As she headed to the bathroom for a long hot bath Katherine's over active mind slowed to a crawl. *After all, what could the bitch do to me? I was going to quit anyway.*

The long hot soak soothed Katherine's aching shoulders and allowed thoughts of her career to drift away. She had successfully negotiated her education and career, her next challenge was to build a private life. Picking up her glass for a last sip, she remembered something Sally had said, "You can't wrap yourself up in an Annual Report and expect it to spark your libido."

Chuckling at Sally's comment and the spirited debate that followed, she decided that after she had given Thomas Sweeney her very best, she'd focus on herself. Finding that special someone to build a life with was a far more difficult challenge. She'd had no luck so far. What she needed to do was figure out why.

11

It was midnight, and Sandra was just disengaging her arms from around Ian's neck, as the last strains of the soft island music died away. When Ian turned towards their table at the quiet corner of the veranda bar, she looked at her watch knowing she had to find an excuse to leave without raising questions. In their few days together, Sandra learned the composed stiff upper lip charmer had a sensitive soul. He continued to delight her without delving into her personal life, seeming to sense those topics she'd consider off limits. With slightly more than two days left she didn't want anything to disturb this idyllic bedmate.

"Darling?" she cooed.

"My Dove?"

The whispered endearment sent shivers down Sandra's spine. "Will you excuse me for a few moments? I promise to be right back"

"Of course. I await your return." Kissing the fingers of her hand, the hand that he had held for the last three dances, Ian slowly released her.

Trying not to seem in a hurry, Sandra kissed Ian on the lips, lingering just long enough to see his interest flare, and his so very sexy smile that said, 'I'm all yours.' "I promise to return with a full and lusty heart."

Once beyond the restaurant, Sandra walked briskly to the business center and the phone, Ian far from her mind.

"Welcome, Ms. Charney," greeted the cheerful business office receptionist. "You wish to place a call to the States?"

"Yes, please." And, settling once again in the small booth, Sandra dialed her secretary. She knew her assistant would be available. Even though it was approaching 6 am in New York, she knew Alice would be getting ready to leave home. Sandra expected her to be in the office before seven when she was out of town. Alice was the one person on this earth she trusted.

"I haven't heard from you. What have you found?"

"Ms. Charney," Alice replied. "I didn't find anything. However, I did find some notes in Ms. Cunningham's desk drawer about Mr. Abbott. His education, age and job history. Nothing of a sensitive nature. She might be working up new bios for the annual report." Alice's crisp reply suited Sandra. Her secretary knew to answer her questions in as few words as possible.

"Nothing? No emails, no new documents?"

"Now that you ask, there were no new documents logged on since Friday. There was some email traffic. Nothing unusual. But, her document directory shows nothing for the beginning of this week. Oh, yes, one thing. Didn't you leave her an assignment?"

"Yes. She was to put together a list of business reporters for interviews with our research team."

"I did find an incomplete media list. It could have been that one. I'll check further and get back to you."

"No. Don't do anything more until I call you." Hanging up without so much as a thank you, Sandra felt something just out of reach. Only a feeling, but like a grain of sand in her shoe it was a consistent mistrust of Katherine Cunningham. What could that usurper be up to? Her job is to research, write, and report only to me. Normally she'd be drafting several documents at any one time. Yet, so far this week she hadn't logged in even one. When she got a minute she'd check into Cunningham's computer from her laptop. Alice must have missed something. I left her enough work to keep a bee-hive busy.

Sandra hurried back to Ian. What she needed was to get Cunningham out of her mind with some heavy, heart-stopping sex.

"Darling," Sandra purred as she approached Ian sipping a cognac in the almost empty outdoor bar. "Why don't we take that to someplace more private?" Seeing the sparkle of mischief flash across Ian's face, Sandra spirits lifted. For now, all was right with her world.

"My dear, what a civilized idea. Maybe, a visit to my bungalow? You haven't seen it. I had a midnight snack sent over just for you."

"You tempt me with food and champagne?"

"Of course. And I believe your favorite snack… dessert."

"My hero." Taking his arm, Sandra's mind focused on the hours ahead during which she would be the center of his universe. This relative stranger answered a deep need, one Sandra sought to fill her entire adult life. She yearned to be treasured. Ian, with all of his formality of posture and expression, was charming and had intuitively wrapped her in the protective cloak of his company. Sandra relished the way he made her feel. With Ian, she forgot the crisp professional woman, clinging to her position with iron-clad control. Ian made her feel younger, smarter, and highly desirable. To Ian she was perfection.

12

If money was the elixir of life, then he was storing a supply of magic promised to make his dreams of wealth, power, and social position come true. Blackmailing Abbott was personal. His reason for living was to amass a fortune of international proportions.

Hunched over his computer in the dimly lit home office, the fifty-year-old diminutive man read the latest entry on his bank statement. Satisfied, he kicked the padded footstool to one side as he rose and slowly circled the room. Thoughts of revenge crowded his mind because today's review of his finances showed that his future was on solid footing. No one would ever tell him what to do again. In the not too distant future, he would open his own investment company and live life as a wealthy expatriate. *I'll join a men's club, circulate with the power players, and then find a model-perfect woman to marry.*

Wouldn't his mother be surprised? She continually told him he'd never amount to anything. "You can't even find a woman who wants to be seen with you. Look at you. You're short, fat; just plain dumpy, and you dress like an actor." To her mind actors were the lowest form of life just above insects. Even though she had been dead for five years, merely thinking of her had him standing taller with shoulders pulled back. He remembered his father's reaction when he'd been caught crying after one of his mother's verbal attacks. "Son, stand straight. A strong back strengthens your nerve."

Why was it that every time he had achieved some measure of success, his mother's words of reproach would echo in his ears. Knowing it was because he looked like his deadbeat father didn't help salve his wounded ego. An actor of moderate skill, Charles Rossini was somewhat of a confidence man. He dressed in sharp suits with brightly colored shirts, and while he may have lacked class, he didn't lack ambition.

Charles Rossini had met a Las Vegas cocktail waitress Alma, who he'd bedded and wedded on impulse after winning the largest poker stake in his life. He wouldn't know that would be the last time he'd win anything.

On one school break he had accompanied his Dad on tour with a traveling theatrical troupe, and watched from the wings as he acted in one small role after another. Never a star, Charles had explained he was considered a character actor.

"Dad, why do you travel so much?" he had asked. "Can't you work at the local Grande Theater? You are always out of town."

"Son, I have to go where the parts are. Acting is the way I support you and your mother. I had hoped you'd follow me on the boards. This summer will be the perfect time for me to begin your training. Just wait, the actresses in this company will love you."

He had been eight-years-old that summer and wanted to be like his Dad--charismatic, popular with the audience and actors alike. Rushing home to tell his mother about his plans, he remembered cringing at her shrill reply. "I'm putting an end to this foolishness. You stay in school. The end!"

But his Dad hadn't kept his word to support his family. When he couldn't find a theater to employ him, he used his actor's skills to sell insurance policies door-to-door. Unfortunately, he was a loser through and through. Married a shrew, couldn't keep a job, loved the ladies, and drank away any money he managed to earn. But certain of his lessons in the importance of appearance had taken root. Thinking of his long road to success, the quiet man thought of the adage that a man dressed for the position he wanted, not the one he had. Now, when he looked in his mirror, he saw a wizard of finance.

Only wealth, the kind you read about on the pages of *The Financial Times*, would free him from his family ghosts and other indignities; the woman he loved, who ignored him...the boss who favored someone else. After years of being an also ran, he was going to emerge triumphant, freed from his pedestrian shackles.

*   *   *

It was after midnight, and his eyes were burning with fatigue. Pouring a cognac from a decanter kept on his side table, he savored the first sip. He never had more than a few sips, fearing he had inherited his father's weakness for alcohol. Closing down his computer, the man's stubby hand placed a flash drive with copies of his financial records, beneath the false bottom of his desk's center drawer. Beyond tired, the multi-millionaire sat back in his chair and closed his eyes, savoring his success.

Images of a mansion with uniformed staff, park-like grounds, and furnishings designed to replicate the elegance he'd seen in real estate brochures, soothed his tired mind. His dream would soon be a reality. Quietly and over a lifetime of scrimping, saving, and scouring the world for investment opportunities, he'd built an empire.

Glancing to the side of his desk, he saw the latest Tiffany & Co. catalogue. He turned to the page he'd marked and looked at a pair of gold and diamond cufflinks. Fingering the photo, he decided they would be his next little purchase. After all, now that his personal assets had reached their first plateau, waiting a year or so more to make his move would add considerably to his fortune.

In the meantime, he needed to look successful. The custom tailored suits, loafers handmade in Italy, and jeweled cufflinks added to his stature. The differences between the man he was and his father were more than in dress. After all, Charles Rossini, the deadbeat actor, wouldn't have known the differences between a flawless diamond and that of zircon. Nor, would he have understood the subtly of wearing navy and grey suits. "Dad, you taught me what not to do. Now, you wouldn't know me if you passed me on the street."

13

Katherine was facing a problem of coordinating data from several online sources in preparation of her Q&A for Mr. Abbott's Friday interviews. Since the surfaces of her credenza and two guest chairs remained clear of handbags, books, files, or clothing, only she was aware of the disorganized bits and pieces of information reverberating in her mind. Switching back and forth between her laptop placed out of sight below her desk and her desktop computer required all of her concentration. Confusing the two assignments would be disastrous.

Katherine's focus was temporarily broken by a shadow in her office doorway. It wasn't a draft that was causing a chill on her arms, it was the sight of Charney's secretary Alice, poised as if to enter. Katherine discreetly closed her laptop while looking up from her desktop monitor.

"Yes, Alice. Come in." Fortunately, the media list was clearly visible on her computer screen. "May I help you?"

Katherine watched as Sandra Charney's assistant tried to be subtle while checking out her office.

"I've heard from Ms. Charney and she asked me to remind you of the last minute assignment she emailed earlier this week."

"Yes?" What was the woman up to trying to look at her monitor, instead of respectfully standing in front of her desk?

"Ms. Cunningham, I noticed you were in a rush last evening, and this is the first chance I've had to stop by. It's just that Ms. Charney is expecting to have that media list and accompanying documents delivered to her home on Friday. If I may be of assistance, please don't hesitate to call."

Shit, it's only Wednesday, and Charney now has her secretary pushing my buttons. Smiling, Katherine took a breath before answering. "Alice, as you can see, I'm working on it. However, I appreciate your offer. I will bring an envelope to your office around 4:30pm on Friday. I know you will make sure Ms. Charney has her information as per her instructions."

Watching as the 52-year-old grey-haired assistant left, Katherine thought not for the first time that if Alice had worked for her, she would have sent her to a salon for a complete hair and makeup consultation. Maybe if Alice looked more modern and less frumpy, she'd be happy with herself and wouldn't slavishly follow the glamorous but frosty Charney, a woman she obviously idolized.

Retuning to focus on her laptop, Katherine reviewed the final list of questions and possible answers she planned to give to Sweeney that afternoon. She wouldn't begin contacting the three reporters to set up Abbott's interviews until late Thursday. For the present, her part in Friday's announcement was on schedule.

As she stretched her arms and legs, Katherine thought about her life. While she loved being included in the corporate intrigue and hoped to prove herself worthy of handling this crisis, she heard her mother's voice admonishing, 'Katherine dear, you must broaden your horizons. Your father and I didn't raise you to confine yourself to an office.'

Mom and Dad, I miss you both. She had always been aware of just how special her parents were, especially since their death two-years earlier. They had been hiking in the Alps when caught in a freak avalanche. Since her dad had retired both had become avid outdoor enthusiasts taking outward bound trips in remote locations around the world.

I couldn't begin to attempt your journeys. I've always been more of a golf and swimming kind of gal, she thought.

They were also different in the way they raised her. She remembered the long hours spent with her college girlfriends, discussing each of their parents' plans for their lives. To a friend, they were being positioned for a safe future first as a teacher, then an early marriage and children. One of her friends said that her mother had hoped she'd find a husband while still a freshman in college. *Yes, Sarah, and when I told you that my mom had said that marriage wasn't for everyone, you were horrified.*

Looking at a framed photo on her desk, she remembered when it had been taken. She had been seventeen and her parents had planned a quick three days in Denmark. There they stood, three smiling faces standing at the entrance to Tivoli Gardens in Copenhagen. Of course as the daughter of an airline pilot, she had traveled to Paris, London, Rome, Copenhagen, Amsterdam, Mexico City, and of course Canada. She had lived the excitement of seeing new places, meeting new people, and learning about cultures different from her own. Her parents had handed her the world. They wanted her to grab it with both hands.

Mom, you would have loved my career. Thinking of all the family dinner table discussions during which she would share her triumphs and defeats, then wait to hear her parents' suggestions. *I wonder what they'd advise now about handling my stifling boss. Mom would probably counsel me to keep my thoughts to myself, my head down, and work my way out of this box. Of course Dad would counsel the importance of taking back control of my job, even if I was under the dominion of a paranoid control freak.*

College had changed her world. Not the course of study, communications, but the professor who had recommended her for the summer position with a New York public relations agency. Katherine remembered being excited about the opportunity, but not understanding why she had been selected for the position. She had no PR experience with previous summer jobs having been a salesgirl at a local department store, and a bookkeeper at an air cargo company.

Upon meeting with the agency's senior vice president, she learned that it was her clearly written analytical reports that convinced him she'd be an ideal candidate for a short-term assignment. *Oh how eager I was. Imagine a real job, something I could begin to build a resume with.*

The agency's president, on seeing her enthusiasm for the assignment, hired her on the spot. He had explained since staffing was tight, they couldn't afford to send a senior member to attend a meeting of scientists being held at the end of the summer in New Orleans. Until then she would be a fact checker and learn the agency's format for preparing summaries of scientific papers. By the end of the summer she would know how he wanted those reports written and was confident she would be prepared to gather information at the meeting in New Orleans.

She could picture her daily commute from Long Island to New York City, dressing every morning in a suit and heels and joining the rush of people to her first real job. It made her feel like an adult, not a co-ed who'd return to campus when the summer was over. During the early weeks at the agency, she'd been put to work collating research from pharmaceutical studies. Then the trip. It had crystallized her parents' teachings, to grab the world with both hands.

Katherine could still feel her excitement when she flew to New Orleans on an afternoon flight after having spent the morning at the office preparing her notes. She hadn't minded the long hours involved because she found life on the road, even for that one overnight trip, an enticing new experience. Her parents weren't there to guide and protect her. She had to remember to keep her packing light, her wallet and airline tickets in her handbag, and not to let her briefcase out of her sight. It hadn't occurred to her that traveling alone might be problematic. After all, by now at the advanced age of 20, travel was second nature. She was looking forward to her first solo adventure.

Katherine chuckled as she remembered telling her parents about the trip and how she'd been met by a limousine for transportation to her hotel. Then there had been flowers waiting in her room along with a note of welcome by the meeting's Chairman. *Dad, you were so funny. You laughed and said, 'Boy, now you are so spoiled, I'll never get you to travel with your mother and me again.'*

The meeting had started at 8 am and kept her busy for twelve hours, right up until she'd left for the airport and her flight back to New York. But the rush of learning about the scientific progress on several drugs had delayed exhaustion. She had been given an insider's glimpse of a possible breakthrough that promised never before anticipated cures for diabetes. It had been her responsibility to accurately write-up the meeting's conclusions. *I had been so revved, I didn't have time to wonder if I'd be up to the job.*

She remembered getting home in the wee hours, and jumping into bed knowing that she'd only get 4 hours of sleep before returning to the office and preparing her report. *Yeah, somehow it got done and turned in before I made it home. By the time my head hit the pillow I was out for a full 12 hours.*

Thinking back on that summer, Katherine realized she had been given the best training for her current position with Marathon where her primary responsibilities were research, writing reports, and speeches. Since graduating with her MBA, she had always felt lucky to have been hired by Marathon. It was a company she admired and was continually fascinated by the research into developing cutting edge products. Even working under Charney hadn't curbed her enthusiasm for learning about the next area of research or introduction of a new product. But, just maybe, it was time to listen to another of her mother's words of wisdom about life. It was one of the topics she and Sally hashed over recently. Why two single, bright, attractive career women couldn't find a suitable man to date, let alone have a lasting relationship with.

Picking up her desk phone, she dialed Sally's office. "Hey, are you free tonight?"

"Sure. What do you have in mind?"

"How about take out at my place. Say seven?"

"I can do that. I'll bring a new bottle of Vodka and Limoncino. See you then."

As Sally hung up, Katherine turned back to the list in front of her. Just a one more article by the last of the six reporters and her work for Charney would be done. How convenient to be able to gather reporters' prior articles via the internet. *Before the internet's access to journalists past work, I'd have spent hours at the library. What a waste of time!*

With Charney's assignment completed, Katherine had a premonition she'd forgotten something important. Fatalistic though that was, things were just going too smoothly. Her warning systems went on alert. *Probably just being my compulsive self*, she thought.

*   *   *

Hugs and kisses greeted Sally as she handed Katherine her purchases. Carrying her friend's coat and tote bag to the hall closet, Katherine led Sally to the kitchen where she proceeded to mix their Limoncino martinis, pouring them into thin stem crystal glasses. "A twist of lemon peel for that last bit of flavor and we can unwind," Katherine said.

Retiring to the living room, Sally sat in the comfy oversized dark blue club chair and raised her glass. "To us."

Katherine sipped to the toast and settled in the matching chair. She kicked off her heels and took her first free breath since she woke that morning. "Sally, do you remember what my mom said about finding a life beyond work?"

"Of course I do. It was so unlike what my parents had planned for me. The only thing they wanted was for me to graduate at the top of my law school class, work for a top-tier law firm and make partner before I turned thirty-four."

"Which, you did."

"Well, junior partner anyway. Becoming a named partner, with my name on the letterhead, is probably not in my future. Unless of course, I open my own law office. But your mom wanted me to have a life filled with love and laughter. That advice simply wasn't in my mother's milk. Why?"

"Well, my world is currently circumscribed by this apartment and work. It's no longer enough. Any suggestions?"

Sally took a sip of her drink before answering. "Katherine, hear me out. We've been friends for years and you have always answered my questions about getting a life outside of work with a quip. You have had an on and off switch on this particular subject. Especially on finding a man, like the ones we dreamed about in college. Why are you thinking about something as important as this now?"

"I'm not content. Something's missing."

"Before we change your life, why not tell me what's really on your mind. And, by the way, when was the last time you even thought about a man in your life?"

"I love my job. You and I have a wonderful friendship. But I miss Noel. Don't misunderstand me, I don't miss his absences, or not putting my needs before his own. I miss the connection with a man I respect. Passion. Feeling safe in his arms."

"You are still dreaming of that guy? Why?"

"Well there were those two years with Noel. At the beginning they were so romantic. He had his career and I was building mine."

"And by the second year?"

"I realized it wasn't going anywhere. And I guess I was so busy, I just accepted it."

"What changed your mind?"

"I was walking home one evening and I saw an older gentleman helping his wife from a taxi. They were both dressed in evening clothes and so wrapped up in each other it was if the rest of the world didn't exist. It was the way he took her arm and the way she leaned into him. I was jealous and hurt that my life with Noel didn't have even a fraction of that warmth and affection. So I got out. I wanted to be cherished not consulted as if I were another business appointment. I wanted love with the sexual passion."

"But you were with him for almost two years?"

"Yeah. I kept hoping he'd change. Outside of fantastic sex, we lived separate lives. I guess I can't separate intimacy from love. Noel apparently wanted things the way they were, separate. Anytime I suggested we get away for the weekend, he always had some excuse. I just stopped trying."

"Congratulations. You shouldn't have put up with him for that long. Why do you think Steven and I never worked out? It wasn't due to incompatibility, it was boredom. I guess my brain wants a companion as much as my body does." Sally said.

"Maybe we see men the way we hope they are until we wake up to reality." Katherine added.

"Guilty."

"So Sally, how about your social life? You're out there and trying. What do you struggle with?"

"I struggle with myself. I told you I have been finding dates using online services. But the truth is that I haven't met anyone who's even a contender for a relationship, let alone marriage."

"Don't you find that when you are introduced to someone by a friend, they are nicer to you than if you met them at some bar? It's like you've been prescreened and approved. So if the guy likes the friend, he is prepared to at least like meeting you. My fear is that the internet is just a fancy bar. You meet and greet like you're in a meat market. I doubt we will meet any real men of interest without a personal introduction."

"But without the internet, how do you plan to even meet someone? All of our mutual friends are women, and no one is currently married or even dating a significant partner. To make matters even more restrictive, we all work long days leaving little time to explore those downtown clubs you read about. I can't imagine leaving a club at 2 am when I have to be up at 5 am and in the office before 7 am."

"My thoughts exactly. That's why I was wondering if any of our girlfriends might know at least one acceptable male." Katherine said.

"I'm not sure, but I know at least three attorneys with Ivy League caliber brothers. Don't you know a couple of women in your PR group?" Sally asked.

"We don't need an army. I was thinking that if I held a dinner party for say twelve or fourteen guests, where each woman had to bring an available and acceptable male, we could expand our circle of potential men. I could bring

Marty, or maybe Michael and you could invite Ben, that financial genius of a brother of yours."

"What a clever idea. What makes you think we could arrange something like that? Every single woman I know searches for dates online. Then there are the speed dating groups. Hardly enough time to make a guesstimate as to whether or not you would actually want to spend more than fifteen minutes with any one of them. Long ago we gave up on meeting anyone of interest in cocktail lounges and local bars. And you know workplace romances are fraught with problems. If they go bad, it isn't the man who gets fired, it's the woman."

"Sally, I've never been tempted by a coworker. However if I ever stepped over that line, Thomas Sweeney would certainly be a candidate. But, realistically, I keep remembering something I heard one of the men at work tell a colleague, 'You don't dip your pen in company ink!'"

"I've never heard that one. Crude, but apt. So since your table only seats six, how would you host twelve people?" Sally asked.

"I'd do a buffet. And, there is enough seating for twelve. I don't want it to be such a large group that the atmosphere is no warmer than a cocktail reception."

"If we plan this far enough in advance, I can help you put it together. We can get the food from one of those gourmet markets you love so much."

"Yes, lasagna, some chicken breasts Florentine, a salad, and desserts. We can do that easily."

"I'm in and will provide the wine. But aren't you overscheduled as it is? What's with that super-secret assignment?"

"The Bitch returns Monday. Who knows, when she hears about what I've been doing, I may have lots of time on my hands. We just have to wait and see if I'm alive long enough to plan a party."

14

ons of bitches! Having just read an email alert from his bank in the Cayman Islands, the crazed man's focus remained glued on the briefly worded message. Each word raised his body temperature another degree.

> Dear Customer – We are writing to alert you to coming changes in the manner in which we oversee accounts held by US citizens. Effective July 2014, we are going to begin reporting activity on each of these accounts to the United States Internal Revenue Service. If this change impacts your relationship with us, we recommend that you contact your bank representative at your earliest.
>
> I assure you that your business is important to us and it is our wish to continue to provide you with the best in personalized customer service.
>
> Sincerely,
> Richard Thompson
> Bank President

Fuck it! So far he had evaded the IRS attempts to identify his off-shore holdings. Realizing that his Cayman bank had no choice but to sign an agreement to disclose US citizen accounts or forfeit their financial access to US markets, he was glad he had already transferred one of his Cayman accounts to Andorra.

OK you bastards. I'll just close the new account with Abbott's $800,000, before the end of the week. The government of the people is beginning to oppress its people.

From what he had been reading early compliance to IRS regulations had been met with a slap on the wrist, whereas the new penalties were draconian. The government was prepared to levy a 30% withholding rate on all dividends and interest. Or, if a person has been found to have willfully withheld information on their tax returns, stiffer penalties could include having their entire off-shore account confiscated, along with being sent to prison.

Closing down his email, he directed his attention to his financial spreadsheets. When his eyes focused on the bottom line total of all four bank accounts, he sat straighter and smiled, savoring the fact he had amassed a fortune of approximately six million dollars. Since the bulk of his assets were invested in securities and real estate, daily fluctuations in market values limited his ability to give a finite total to his growing wealth. For the time being, it was gratifying to know that most all of his millions were safely tucked away in Andorra, an additional sum to follow shortly. *Then it's good bye Cayman Islands. Hello independence.*

An intense, dapper, middle aged man, he began building his future while a freshman in college, opening his first bank account in New York City, with $100 he'd earned editing classmates' college papers. As he moved up the business ladder going from one job to the next, he continued to use this as his bank of record. Now, as a senior executive in his company, all paychecks and bonuses were deposited to this account, withdrawing funds as needed to pay for normal living expenses. He considered both his job and bank account as necessary distractions to his primary focus of plotting and planning for his future life abroad.

Reading a print out of his New York bank statement, he saw the regular withdrawals for personal expenses and for payments to the US Treasury, New York State and New York City, taxes on his salary. He was surprised the government allowed him to keep anything of his annual $250,000 salary. *Enough is enough! Soon you won't be getting any more from me.*

The next printout depicted personal investments made from a second bank account in the name of VC Futures, Limited. Established in Andorra to trade international stocks and derivatives, this account too was building nicely and so far without the prying eyes of the US Treasury. To make doubly sure that this account and all correspondence remained untraceable, he'd set up an email account with an online provider based in Hong Kong. In that online community he was simply another day trader, like so many other ambitious men around the world.

The following printout was of his third offshore account, VC Properties, Limited, a second account located in Andorra. It was this account that was the repository of his real estate portfolio that would someday be the corner stone of his expanded investment operations. The beauty of this account, as with his brokerage account, was that it too was managed entirely online. Believing in the adage that pennies grew into nickels, and nickels grew into dimes, and so forth, had over the years served as his philosophy by which he purchased and sold lots small enough not to draw the attention of real estate watchdogs. In the future, he planned to create investment partnerships for billion dollar real estate deals, not these tokens-on-a-game-board of finance. After he moved the newer Cayman account of $800,000 to Andorra, only the New York account would be in possible jeopardy from IRS scrutiny.

He had thought long and hard about where he would retire. He required a friendly banking system, an international population, and a society that appreciated artistic and social amenities. In short one that drew an international crowd of powerful people. He had visited Andorra on vacation and found it offered an appealing way of life that met all his conditions. Alternative locations he'd considered included Cyprus and the Cayman Islands. He had decided long before this new attention by the IRS that he wanted a location less well known. So he'd zeroed in on Andorra, a country so small as to be relatively unknown.

Six million dollars was nothing to sneeze at. But it was small potatoes in the world he wanted to join. Once established in Andorra, he planned to increase this sum significantly. He'd be a man to know…noteworthy in the only way that mattered, for his wealth. *Dad, I hope you have been watching from Hell. I have real money and I plan to get more!*

Lighting a custom rolled cigar, he took a puff and realized that anger at the father who had died ten years before, no longer ruled his life. Pleased with the balancing of his accounts, he took another puff and rolling the cigar back and forth in his stubby fingers, smiled. His future was on track. Soon he would make up for all the years of slights and begin the life he deserved. Yes, he was one of his best creations.

15

Megan had been in the study, sitting with legs curled up on the sofa, watching her husband stare into space. "Sweetheart? We have to have a serious plan of action. We can't leave it all to Uncle Thomas. Let's put our heads together. Maybe we can find some bit of information that will help resolve this crisis."

Looking at his wife, Edward was bewildered by her take charge attitude. Megan was by far the easiest person to be with of anyone he'd ever known. It wasn't as if he had dated a lot of women. But Megan was in a class all by herself. Not only was she lovely with her redhead's complexion and soft strawberry blonde hair, she was spot on smart. As an under graduate at Harvard, she had honed her mind on numbers, from pick-up card games to figuring the odds of a particular stock. If he didn't know her better, he'd have thought she was raised by a gambler, not staid Thomas Sweeney. His wife was a treasure, and he adored her from the first moment they met. But he wouldn't consider her someone to step up for a fight.

Puzzled, Edward sat at his overly organized desk, waiting for her to continue. He had been mulling over his predicament all morning, reviewing the meeting they had attended the night before. Thomas had put plans in place to handle his resignation. He even planned to hire a private investigator to retrace his steps on that fateful evening. What else was there to do? Edward was at a loss, no matter how hard he tried he couldn't remember how he'd gotten into this jam. He felt shamed and impotent.

"Edward, pay attention. Look, it's Wednesday, we have two more days to help Thomas track this blackmailer down. I won't even think of the consequences if he can't."

"Megan dear, last evening Thomas put his plan of action in place. To my mind he chose well in enlisting Katherine to announce my retirement. I don't like or trust Sandra Charney to do what is best for me. Her total focus is on keeping the company clear of any scandal. Katherine on the other hand is a solid professional and while loyal to the company, she has a humanity that makes me more comfortable taking her advice. From what I saw last evening, she genuinely wants to help us."

He watched as Megan walked over to him, reached down, and turned his head to face her. "Sweetheart, Marathon's plan to announce your retirement is a solid one, and I agree Katherine is best at implementing it. But I want to kill that bastard who set you up. Only you and I can try to figure out who that might be. I'm convinced that it has to be someone you know, or at least knows you."

Finally facing the truth that his wife was more on top of their predicament than he could be in light of his extreme embarrassment, Edward, decided she was right. "OK. Just where do you want to begin?"

"I don't think this is all about forcing you to fork over $800,000. Why not $1 million? $2 million? This creep knows you can access more. So why didn't he ask for more? I think it's personal. He wants you discredited. If I'm right, we have to trace back years of your life for that one person who wants to do more than destroy your reputation."

"I see your point. But you know I don't pay much attention to people, that's your strength. I just study the numbers. So what can I tell you?"

"OK. How about college? Or law school? Do you remember anything or anyone who might wait years before they attacked you?"

"Come on, Megan, starting with grade school, I've always had a job. How could I remember any of my classmates? All I did was rush from grade school to Mr. Lewis's grocery store to keep his books. When studying at law school became all consuming, Mr. Lewis set aside every Saturday to work with me. Doing his books and those of a couple of his friends, was my life."

When Edward's was seven-years-old, his dad had a heart attack and passed away. Even as a young boy Edward had taken it upon himself to step up and help his mother keep the family together.

Looking at Megan, Edward shook his head. "When Thomas recruited me just out of law school, he sent me to Iowa. In fact while working for Thomas I kept the same hours I had all my life. In Iowa, I was both legal counsel and chief accountant, and in my spare time I studied New York law so I'd be equipped to take over as CFO, when the company made its move to New York. It's sad, but I don't remember even one of my classmates from the age of seven."

"Edward, I know how hard you worked. Your sister told me she and your brothers had always felt guilty about how you gave up everything to help them out."

"It was the only way. In addition to working to pay for college and law school, I tried to see they had extra funds."

"Sweetheart, your devotion enabled them to grow into happy and successful adults."

"Yes. Cindy is a successful speech therapist and Jimmy and Paul are both CPA's. Maybe we should give Jimmy a call, after all he's a forensic accountant with the FBI. Or, Paul, he's a partner with a small and growing accounting firm."

"You see. We have alternatives. However, that's still down the road. First we have to go over everyone you work with. Maybe something will occur to you."

Giving his wife a quick kiss, Edward was reminded once again how lucky he was to have found this smart, warm and loving woman. "OK. Where do we start?"

"So, no one stands out from those years at school. It must be something more recent. Did you fire anyone at Marathon? Someone, who might want to get even?" Megan asked.

"No. In fact when I started working for Thomas there weren't too many of us on staff. There was Thomas, his friend and head of research, Dr. Shen Lu, later Victor Rosso, and by the time we were ready to move to New York, I had recommended they hire Jeremy Irving as Senior Counsel so I could focus on the company's financials. When we were small, I was able, with the assistance of a local Iowa law firm, to stay on top of trademark, patent, and liability law. But as we grew, just protecting our newly developed nutraceuticals had become a full time job."

"The link must have been forged after Marathon's move to New York City. You, Shen, Victor, Jeremy and Thomas were all the senior management at that time?"

"Yes. Sandra joined us in the new offices a little while later, and Phil McKinnon was hired to work with Jeremy. He had just passed his New York Bar exam and loved patent law. I knew he would be someone both Jeremy and I could work with. I was right."

"OK. No, to Jeremy or Phil. How about Shen Lu? How did you get along during those early research discussions? Was there anything you did to curb or prevent any of his research? I gather he can get into some rather obtuse areas. Think back to see if there was ever anything you've done that might cause him problems?"

"We've always worked from the same point of view. Shen is very thrifty with Marathon's funds. In fact the future of Marathon is closely tied to Shen's work in trying to perfect his great grandfather's formulas. So far he has replicated three that have been market leaders and strengthened our niche in what is becoming a very crowded category. Anyway, I thought you liked the man. Isn't he almost family? He may seem inscrutable, but I've found him warm and interesting to be with."

"Yes, Love, I've always liked Shen. Thomas use to bring him home and we'd all have dinner together. I especially loved the stories he told about life during his great grandfather's time in China. He painted his tales of China so clearly they brought his great grandfather to life."

Reaching out Megan gave Edward's shoulder a little squeeze. "Sweetheart, you are part of the Sweeney family. You shared in those dinner conversations with Shen and Uncle Thomas even before we were married. Shen is part of our family."

"Who else is on that calculating brain of yours? I must admit I rarely see this side of you." Edward said.

"And why would you? I leave all that calculating to you," Megan quipped. "So, now to Victor. How do you get on with my former boss? You never mention him. Is it because I worked with him at the time we met?"

"I'm never comfortable around him. It isn't anything he's done or said. It's the man himself. You worked directly for Victor. What's your impression?"

"You know that I left my public relations job to work for Uncle Thomas at the time of the company's move to New York. You were still in Iowa finishing up. I would never have met you if it hadn't been for that reception Uncle Thomas threw to announce the company's move." Looking at his wife, Edward felt her love as strong now as when they met.

"Anyway, Victor was looking for an assistant who could manage the books. Thomas needed someone personally loyal to him. So, I agreed. With my MBA and talent with numbers, my place was to help design record keeping systems so they would accommodate future growth. Victor was the detail-minded executive charged with responsibility for making sure Thomas's visions were implemented. Actually, in my capacity as Victor's assistant I could study every aspect of the company, from how Marathon processed its raw ingredients into our high quality products, to how we would distribute them worldwide. Even then Thomas was keeping his eye on every aspect of his baby."

"Did you like, even respect the man?"

"Victor?"

"Yes. I guess I want to know what you thought working with the man."

"I never thought of Victor in those terms. He did what he did, and I took care of the details. It just seemed to work."

"In my case, while I worked directly with Victor as well as with Shen, Phil, and Sandra, I was hired by Thomas and reported only to him. I have always kept myself somewhat apart from most of the staff. Mainly because I was charged with overseeing all department budgets, I had to be ready to question or make cuts regardless of who presented their case for additional funds."

"Well what about Ms. Charney? How do you get along with that witch? She's one cold woman, missing a piece of humanity."

Taking hold of his wife's hand, Edward replied, "You've got Sandra all wrong. If you look into her employment history you will see that she had tenaciously built a career of excellence before Thomas hired her to represent the firm. Did you know she started out as an assistant to a marketing executive? In the days when assistant was a euphemism for secretary? Anyway, she worked her way up to vice president of that agency in a record five years. Of course she was younger then, and appeared a bit softer, but in all these years she has lived up to her early references. She has a particular facility with communicating our story. She has also proved invaluable at keeping Marathon's news coverage limited to our successes."

"Do you trust her?"

"Yes, if the company is at stake. But, she seems to be single minded about her responsibilities, and I find her to be tedious company. She reminds me of a closed book. Something chiseled in stone and not amenable to change." Looking at Megan, Edward sighed. "I guess that leaves Victor as a suspect."

"For now. Let's see, I had worked for him for about three years before we got married. I remember Victor wasn't too happy about my leaving when we married. Imitating Victor's tone, she recalled that conversation. 'Megan, you are making a big mistake. You are smart and have a strong future here. I've already promoted you from manager to Assistant Vice President of Operations. You could replace me if you stayed.'"

Kissing her husband, she whispered, "Sweetheart, it was no contest. I'd follow you anywhere."

Thinking a bit more clearly, Edward tried to recap what Megan had told him about her announcing their engagement to Victor. "Megs, after you told Victor we were engaged, did he treat you any differently? Anything that might suggest we investigate him, or at least go over his records?"

"What are you thinking? That Victor, that peacock has the balls to set you up and exhort $800,000? Hardly."

"What I'm asking for is a reading on that man. He's so obsequious."

"Why are you suddenly suspicious of Victor?"

"Because I don't believe I have ever gone out of my way to make an enemy. Of all the senior staff, Victor is the only one who has kept his distance from me. The others respect the difficulty of the chief financial officer to keep tabs on the bottom line. Yet I would happily have dinner with Shen and Phil, a man-to-man kind of evening. While I don't think I could include Sandra, we have always worked well together. Victor is another matter. I couldn't have dinner with him. I wouldn't even know where to begin a conversation. In all these years of working with the man, I don't know anything about him."

"Edward, in all the time I've worked for him I'd never seen him do anything that could be considered improper. He is a bit of a showoff. He has to make people feel he's important. I believe he comes from humble beginnings. That may have something to do with his personality."

"And I was born with a wooden spoon, unlike yours of gilt." He often teased Megan that she didn't know what it was like to be poor. He swore that she never would.

"It doesn't show on you. Edward, my love, you are the epitome of an accomplished leader. One look at you and people see success. They instinctively know you are trustworthy and would be honorable in anything you did."

Standing up and enfolding Megan in his arms, Edward heaved a sigh. "I wish I had a magic wand and could make this all go away." Releasing her, Edward held her a bit away, hands resting lightly on her waist. "I don't think Victor would do anything to you, my Darling. You're Thomas's niece. You would be out of bounds."

"That didn't stop you, my Love."

"But then I met you at a company reception and didn't know who you were. And, how in the world, once I'd caught sight of you was I to ever get you out of my heart?"

"So I guess Victor is on top of the list of suspects." Megan surmised.

"Since we're talking about the arrogant little man, you should know that he never looks me directly in the eye. In all of our conversations, he always looked aside." Edward said.

"Why not call Uncle Thomas and have his detective look into Victor. His background, and anything else he can find. Maybe he won't find anything, and we will have to continue looking for suspects from people who have crossed your path." Megan added,

"I'll call Thomas. He's known Victor longer than we have. He may be able to provide the private investigator with additional details about the man. Edward made a note to place Victor on top of the list of suspects, primarily for what they didn't know about him, not for anything specific."

16

"**S**hit!" Katherine's mind temporarily blank was unaware of having squeezed the paper cup now dripping coffee on her desk. She just stared at the glow of her computer monitor. What in Hell was it doing on? She always closed it down, even when she left the building for a rare lunch. What a way to live. Always on guard against snoops.

With a renewed sense of caution, and remembering the notepad with information on Edward Abbott in her desk drawer, Katherine wiped the spill, sat at her computer, and began checking it to see if anything had been disturbed. All files were intact and date stamped to the last time she had opened them. She didn't find any signs of someone having accessed her files. She may have forgotten the notepad, but knew she'd never forget to turn off her computer.

Opening her desk drawer, she saw the notepad was exactly where she had left it. Breathing easier, Katherine ripped the pages with her notes on Abbott and put them in her tote bag. Just to make sure there were no traces, she ripped the next four blank pages, tore them into shreds, and threw them in her waste basket. *I've been reading too many detective stories. Next I'll be dusting my computer for fingerprints.*

Before she could check her mail or think of her plans for the day, her personal cell phone rang. "Ms. Cunningham, Mr. Sweeney would like to see you. Now if it's possible."

"Of course, Mrs. Tunney, I'll be right up." Grabbing her folio and locking her tote bag with laptop in the credenza behind her desk, Katherine headed for the stairs. Marathon occupied three floors in the office building, and working on the lowest of the three, Katherine had been walking up one flight before taking the executive elevator to Sweeney's office. It was another evasive action meant to keep her activities from any prying eyes. *Shit. If I'm serious about losing a few pounds, I should always take the stairs.*

The floor in between hers and the executive floor, was used as a library and file room. During her normal day she'd spend time in the file room researching information for one of her assignments. Research wasn't a favored chore, so of course Charney always gave those assignments to her.

*　　　*　　　*

Thomas Sweeney greeted her from behind his cleared desk. Thinking of the orderly office, Katherine remembered that even in his home, everything had its place. She was beginning to expect his conversations were equally focused on one thing at a time. Indicating that she sit in the chair across from him. Katherine relaxed and waited. She wasn't expecting anything more than a discussion about finalizing the Abbott announcement.

"Katherine. I am going to ask you to help my private investigator in tracking down this blackmailer. I realize this is in no way part of your responsibilities to the company. I am hoping, however, it is in keeping with the spirit of loyalty you have already exhibited to this mission."

Shifting to sit forward on her chair, afraid she'd miss something, Katherine took a moment before she replied. "Mr. Sweeney, I really want Mr. Abbott's situation to be resolved so he can reclaim his life. Of course with no one outside our close group learning anything about the entire wretched incident. But how do you think I can assist your investigator?"

"And you want to know if I am asking you to do anything illegal?"

Katherine's face was beginning to feel uncomfortably warm. He certainly picked up on her reluctance. What would Sally advise? So far she hadn't been asked to do anything illegal. "Yes, that thought did enter my mind. However, I really would like to help. The least I can do is to meet this man and find out how he thinks I could help with his investigation."

"I appreciate your willingness to at the least speak with him. And for understanding just how crucial it is to limit the number of people involved in our plan."

Katherine agreed the fewer people involved in uncovering the source of this plot the safer Sweeney was in keeping it from becoming public knowledge. The fact that Sweeney had even thought to include her in the investigation, was at once an extreme compliment, and a worry. *Well, in for a penny in for a pound,* she decided.

The man I would like you to meet, who by the way is a childhood friend, is someone I'd trust with my life. So I am not going to introduce you to someone with criminal tendencies. His name is John Sparks. Now that you have agreed to hear him out, he would like you to meet with him this morning for a private conversation. If you feel safe in assisting him, it would make me feel more at ease. I believe that whatever you do, your actions will be undertaken with the strictest of caution."

"Yes, Mr. Sweeney, I'm happy to meet Mr. Sparks. If I have any questions, I'll get back to you."

"I think working as closely as we are on this crisis entitles you to call me Thomas. It would make me more comfortable." He said.

What a strangely intriguing concept. Almost like partners or friends, she thought.

Thomas Sweeney handed Katherine a note with John Sparkey's name, address, and time scheduled for the meeting.

One half hour from now? "I'm not sure I can get downtown in this amount of time, Mr. err, Thomas. Traffic is wicked."

"I have a taxi waiting downstairs. It's a normal yellow cab, one I use myself on occasion. Just give Jerry the address and he will charge the trip to my account."

Thomas Sweeney stood, while Katherine remained seated. "Katherine?"

"I have to pick up my laptop and close down my computer. I found it on this morning. Yes, then I can meet Mr. Sparks. But I may be a little late."

Moving to stand over Katherine, Sweeney's low voice had the ring of steel, "You said your computer was on when you got in this morning?"

Looking directly into the clenched face of the man was unnerving. "Yes. I thought it odd. I would normally never leave it on when I'm out of the office. Certainly not overnight." Katherine was focused on what she had to do before meeting with the private investigator and hadn't been aware of speaking aloud. Sweeney's furrowed brow reminded her she had also been unnerved by the incident.

"Katherine, have any of our conversations or drafts of the announcement been entered on your office computer?"

"No, sir. I have been using my laptop which I carry in my tote bag or have locked in the credenza behind my desk. In fact the lock on the cabinet is tricky so if anyone had tried to open it, I would have noticed new scratches on the wood."

"You have to keep away from using all office equipment. Remember, no one must know what we are doing."

Shit! Have I made a serious error? I have been so very careful. I can't do anything to disappoint Thomas.

"Don't worry about the time. I will let Mr. Sparks know you'll be a little late. And Katherine, I have just decided to install a camera in your office. By the time you get back, Mrs. Tunney will be able to see anyone entering or leaving the area."

Breathing a sigh of relief that she wasn't being accused of having been sloppy. Katherine was about to relax, then realized she was being pulled into something more nefarious than the simple preparation of a corporate retirement announcement. First blackmail and a sex video, now her office would be under surveillance. What had she gotten involved in?

Just as Katherine returned to her floor, she saw Alice rounding the corner of desks a few feet away. Something about her even being in the area was unsettling. Alice worked on the other side of the floor where Sandra Charney ruled from a corner empire of apartment-size proportions.

Entering her office, Katherine checked her computer and finding nothing unusual, closed it down. Next, she unlocked her credenza, removed her laptop, and checked to see if anything had been disturbed. Because she spent most of her daily life at the office, Katherine kept personal files including tax returns, legal papers concerning her apartment, financial statements from her brokerage account, and her employment contract. When hiring her, Charney had made it clear she had to fulfill all her contractual responsibilities. She was so specific Katherine kept a copy of the contract on hand, just in case she had reason to question one of Charney's directives. If she had learned anything, it was that contracts were meant to protect the author, not the individual agreeing to the stated conditions.

*   *   *

The taxi let Katherine off at an older office building located on the west side of Manhattan. Entering the nondescript lobby she approached a uniformed security guard complete with badge and radio. A wall directory listing the building's tenants hung behind his desk. Looking for the Sparks & Sons Investigations, Katherine found she was to go to the ninth floor. She was surprised she wasn't required to sign in with the guard or open her tote bag for his inspection. Since 9/11 that seemed to be the protocol in most office buildings throughout the city. Looking toward the ceiling, she spotted a camera. *So another video record of my life. What's next, a tap on my home phone?*

Taking the elevator was an experience in itself as it was no larger than a closet in her New York sized apartment. Emerging from the confined space, she spotted the door to Mr. Sparks' office directly ahead. Greeting her was a receptionist straight out of the 1960's. Pale complexion, dark red lipstick and a matronly figure stuffed into a cardigan sweater set.

All she needs is a string of pearls, Katherine thought as she stopped at the woman's desk. "Hello. I'm Katherine Cunningham I believe I'm expected."

"Certainly." The receptionist picked up the phone, and Katherine heard herself being announced.

"Mr. Sparks is expecting you. Go right in Miss."

Miss? How old was this woman? Thank God for her parents raising her as a person who happened to be a female. Men didn't address one another by Mister, so why did this woman have to call her Miss.? Her name would be more appropriate. She was accustomed to working in a male dominated universe. Yes, she addressed Thomas Sweeney as Mr. Sweeney, or had until this morning. That was correct. He was her senior in age and position. But between women, except for Ms. Sandra Charney of course, it was never Ms., Miss or Misses.

As Katherine walked into the spare masculine office, she wondered, if the secretary out front was an indication of the man she was about to meet, another throwback to the sexist style and manners of the 60s.

The cream walls and undraped windows were so typically masculine! Then Katherine's eyes focused on the blond, very good looking man, standing in greeting. Dressed in grey glen plaid jacket and grey slacks he looked as comfortable as a friendly uncle.

"Ms. Cunningham I'm John Sparks and I am very glad you agreed to meet with me. If I understand Thomas, you will be most helpful in resolving this crisis."

Well, he's direct, if nothing else, Katherine thought. "Mr. Sparks, I don't know how I may be of assistance in this mess, but I do want to help you apprehend this blackmailer and restore Mr. Abbott's reputation."

"Thomas said you were his moral equivalent. So, let me tell you where we are and how I think you may be of assistance."

"I must caution you that I haven't as yet decided to help you, only to hear you out."

"Well said. Ms. Cunningham, I have found the missing footage from the video, and am in the process of trying to identify the girl, and clues to locating the blackmailer."

"You found the photographer? And he or she knows who the client is?"

"Yes and no. The videographer is someone recommended to me by a man I have worked with before. However, the kid who did the filming never met his client. He knows what he did was illegal and agreed to help me locate the girl if I would keep him out of trouble."

"Mr. Sparks, just how can I be of help?" Katherine wanted a clear idea of her role in his search for answers.

"Actually, I was hoping you could tell me about the people in the company who may or may not want to harm Mr. Abbott."

"But I don't work for him. In fact, my boss insists that I don't communicate with any of the senior executives."

"Really? Ms. Cunningham, before you were hired for Ms. Charney's department, hadn't you briefly held a position in other departments? Maybe met a wider group of Marathon executives?"

"Actually, it was during my last year in graduate school. I was a college intern hired as an all-around gofer and worked primarily in one area, Operations. So my knowledge of company employees was limited."

"Who did you come in contact with?"

"Well, I worked under Mr. Rosso's assistant, Megan. Oh, she's Mrs. Abbott now." *I've got to pay attention to what and who he asks me about. Especially if he wants information on the former Megan Sweeney.* Trying not to fidget, she continued, "I didn't notice anything out of the ordinary, except Mr. Rosso wasn't a very pleasant man to work for. I tried to go to Mrs. Abbott for help as much as possible so I wouldn't have to bother him."

"What was there about him that you avoided? Did he make a play for you?"

"It wasn't anything definite. I was only there for one summer. He was just odd."

"Odd?"

"Well, he was abrupt, self-involved, and he strutted. I guess I've never been comfortable around someone who was so self-important. While he never exhibited what I would call a temper, he always demanded attention issuing orders as if he was the only person who mattered. It was much easier to work with Mrs. Abbott."

"Did you work with or were you around any other executives during that period?"

Thinking back some eight years, Katherine tried hard to visualize the company. "Well, at that time Mr. Rosso's office was on the executive floor, at the opposite end of the floor from Mr. Sweeney. While everything I needed was in Mr. Rosso's area, I did sometimes work with other secretaries on that floor. Except for Mr. Sweeney's that is. You know, to deliver reports and such. I seem to remember Sandra Charney. However she usually stayed out of sight, behind office doors. My impression was one of a cool, competent executive. Other than that, most executives just came and went, leaving their assistants to handle their assignments."

"May I be direct? Tell you something that I have been muddling over, and ask for your honest opinion?"

"Of course, Mr. Sparks. I told Mr. Sweeney I wanted to help if I could."

"I believe this situation is personal, maybe a longstanding grudge. The blackmailer requested a remarkably small amount of money in light of Mr. Abbott's access to the Sweeney Family Foundation's funds. I am also beginning to think he is someone from the company."

"In that case, don't you think Mr. Sweeney might be a better person to question?"

"Normally I would. However, he can't go into departments and chat up secretaries or go to the archives and check out the files. I believe you could without raising any suspicion."

Katherine knew she could do most anything except speak to senior executives without raising Charney's ire. "I see. Yes. I am always in the file room. Ms. Charney has me do all the department's research. How would that help your investigation? What would I look for?" Totally confused, hoping this was all Mr. Sparks needed of her. She was all ears, only too happy to search the files for information if it would clear up this disaster.

"It's a funny thing about records. They seem so sterile. In fact, most of my cases have been broken by seemingly insignificant pieces of paper. A listing of suppliers. An accounting for a particular job. A fact in an employee's employment history. A niggling bit of information that by itself is harmless and in light of our problem could be a key to its solution."

"I see. You would have to tell me what to look for. The record room covers nearly half of the 19th floor. Without knowing where to begin, it could take days."

"We don't have days, Ms. Cunningham. If you agree to search the files for me, I will guide you to those areas we need to look at. When I have more specific information, may I get back to you?"

"Yes. Mr. Sparks. I'll get you access to the company files if it will help you ferret out the blackmailer. As you know, I am working off-grid, so please don't contact me at the office." Seeing his reassuring smile was one thing. But still, she was going to check with Thomas before she went any further.

Writing her contact information on a piece of her memo paper, Katherine handed it to him. "I really don't trust my office to be leak proof. This is my home number along with my personal cell should you wish to reach me. If it is an emergency, please have Mr. Sweeney's secretary get in touch."

"Thank you Katherine. I appreciate your willingness to help us find this rat."

17

It had been a little over a week since he'd delivered the video and note to Edward Abbott, demanding payment of $800,000. The threat that if he didn't pay, the video would be released to the tabloid press, had worked. The speed with which Abbott had delivered the funds had him chuckling. He didn't care where Abbott had gotten that amount of money but suspected it hadn't come from his personal bank account or investments. Grinning with glee, the small round figure felt that whatever the repercussions, they'd certainly taint the saintly Abbott's reputation. Mr. Straight and Narrow was now, and would forever, be seen as a crook.

The computer screen confirmed the deposit of $800,000 to his remaining Cayman Island numbered account where it was already accruing interest. Together with the $200,000 he used to open the account, he now had an additional $1 million in cash. Liquidity had always been a weak point in managing his investments. While he tried to keep at least 10% cash in his Andorra accounts, this windfall provided funds for the financial freedom he had worked long and hard to achieve. Instead of having to sell a property or investment, he could use cash for down payments on his new life. If cash was king, he was at least a Duke.

Rubbing his hands together, he refocused and checked his other accounts. One of his Andorra accounts now handled his international real estate holdings, while another, older account was dedicated to investments in stocks, bonds, and other fiscal instruments including arbitrage of foreign currency.

After analyzing his assets, he began pacing around the dimly lit library. It was late evening and his mind was totally absorbed in figuring out how to gain access to a new technology that made hiding money from the government easier. The government was tracking down all US citizens with off-shore bank accounts. *Not mine, you crooks. This time next year you won't even know I exist.*

His palms began to itch. It had been a month ago when by accident he had overheard a conversation with a customer at a downtown electronics store he frequented. The purpose of his visit was to purchase a new smart phone that would provide international access to phone, internet, and email accounts. He wanted to use the phone as his office until he'd finally moved his business to Andorra. As he began to look over the smart phones on the retailer's display, he overheard a life changing conversation. The two men were discussing ways to get $10 million dollars out of the country.

With the purchase no longer on his mind, he listened intently as Miguel explained how the man might arrange the purchase of an astonishing item. It had been a shock to learn of something that even with his international banking experience, he had never heard about. He remembered looking over to the store owner's son and waving a manufacturer's brochure signaling that he had to leave. He was in a hurry, his mind abuzz with this new way to hide money. In all his planning he never imagined an arrangement like this would be so simple. With access to this little item, he could hide the $800,000 and speed up his departure, leaving his unbearable everyday life behind.

18

"Shen, can you come into the city and meet me for lunch?" Thomas Sweeney wanted the assistance of his oldest and best friend. "I know it's an inconvenience, what with your current research winding down. We can meet at my home, let's say 12:30. I just can't make it out to New Jersey right now."

"Of course. If I leave now, I can make the 10:30 train to the city. That should give me plenty of time."

"I hate to make you take this trip. But there is something I need you to do for me. And, it can't be discussed via the usual channels."

"Thomas? I hope you know if there is anything I can do you only have to ask."

"Yes, my friend. I never doubted that you would be there for me. We have a long history of watching out for each other."

"There's a darkness I sense in your voice. You're not ill?"

"Healthy as a man twenty-years younger. It's just that I'm under a bit of a thunder cloud. More about that at lunch." Rushing to end the call, he added, "Shen, there is so much to talk about. I don't want to alarm you but your wise counsel is what I need at the moment."

"Till lunch." Shen replied.

Hanging up on his friend, Thomas was so very glad he had Shen in his life. Since Lucy's death, Shen had been the only one able to keep him in focus. *Darkness in my voice, and in my soul old friend.*

*　　*　　*

Greeting his longtime friend with a warm hand shake, Thomas led Shen into the dining room where a seafood salad plate and tea waited at a small table set for two. He wished this were just a friendly meeting, but no, he needed his friend's assistance.

"Ah, white tea. Are we celebrating something?" Shen asked.

"Unfortunately no."

As Thomas poured the tea from an antique tea pot, he remembered Shen having promised it would bring out the very best in the tea leaves. It had been a gift from Shen when they began the company shortly after their return from military service. Ever since Thomas served his friend this special blend, a kind of personal tea ceremony of friendship. Shen didn't drink wine or hard liquor. He often said that his brain provided enough of a rush that he didn't need either alcohol or drugs for stimulus.

Moving to the table, Shen pulled out a chair, and sitting down, looked up at his friend. "You look tired."

Thomas knew that the physician in Shen would notice something off kilter. He would read tension simply by the appearance of his face or the way he held his body.

"If you have time, I would recommend you see our favorite acupuncturist. Or, if time is short, I could bring in my needles and relieve some of that internal heaviness." Shen said.

Taking his seat opposite Shen, Thomas unfolded his long frame and sat back, feet flat on the floor, hands folded in his lap. "What a simple solution for a very complex problem. Shen, right now I need that active mind of yours. While you enjoy your lunch, let me tell you a story. When I'm done, maybe you will be able to help me resolve at least part of my dilemma."

Picking up his fork and taking a bit of salad, Shen said, "I am assuming this is company related?"

Nodding in agreement, Thomas took a sip of tea, moistening his mouth. It was dry, causing his words to stick. "Edward has gotten himself and the company into an extremely difficult jam. He was tricked and filmed in a compromising position. In order to obtain the original film and not have the information sent to the media, he was told to pay this blackmailer $800,000. Not having the funds, Edward appropriated the money from the Foundation."

"Edward? I can't believe it."

"Me either. Nor, can Edward. He can't even remember how he had been tricked into going into a hotel room and being photographed in bed with this woman."

"We can replace the funds quietly. I can provide half the amount from my savings. Can you get the balance?"

"I can't ask you to rob your retirement fund, Shen. But, yes, I can get at least half from a trust fund I set up long ago for Megan. She doesn't even know it exists. Since it's handled by my personal attorney, he can make a wire transfer into the Foundation without anyone being the wiser."

"Ok. I will call your attorney and I'll get the details for transferring $400,000 to the Foundation. Thomas, I'll do it today. That should take care of the funds. But we still have to find the blackmailer."

"Agreed. Now to tickling you're so very fertile mind. Who would know that Edward could tap that amount of money so easily? A friend, family member, acquaintance?"

"Edward is as closed mouth about the company's finances as he is about his own. He once told me that having been poor was excellent training for having money. He had learned not to give his trust easily. That if strangers, even acquaintances, knew he was wealthy, he would become a target. He also told me something shortly after we began working together that has stuck in my mind. He said that money doesn't hug back. I remember because it showed me that he had his priorities in order."

"I agree. In spite of his rather tough life, he has an honor about him that engenders loyalty."

"In light of what I know about him, it would be my guess that someone at Marathon has targeted Edward for destruction. Someone he may know. Thomas, I can't believe I just said that. I work with the same people Edward does, and I trust them all. But, if I'm right, how do we find this traitor?"

"I agree with you, and Sparkey is leaning in that direction as well. I was hoping that we might provide him with a couple of possible candidates."

"The only people with information about the Foundation are you, myself, Megan, Edward and Victor. We can rule everyone out but Victor. However, I wonder if he's bright enough to hide a crime as blatant as this one." Shen said.

"My friend, you have always underestimated the man. Our operations have become so complex that only a bean counter, I believe that is how you refer to him, can keep everything on track. He leaves your research alone doesn't he?"

"Not entirely. He is always nickel and diming me about my requests for a new piece of equipment, or reimbursement for a trip to study some foreign ingredient. However unpleasant, he does keep out of my work. I consider dealing with him a character-building experience."

As Shen picked at his salad, Thomas remained quiet. The kind of silence of friends comfortable in each other's company.

"Thomas, do you have someone to look over the books? Someone we can trust? It's just that we are so isolated from the organization at large. For which my friend, I sincerely thank you."

"We wouldn't be Marathon without you Shen. I will always protect your independence. Why your books?"

"If this traitor is within the company maybe blackmail is only one of his crimes?" Shen said.

"Interesting idea. Do you know Katherine Cunningham?" She works for Sandra."

His lunch forgotten, Shen replenished their tea. "Yes, she comes out to see Seth when working on an announcement or speech concerning one of our pet projects. While I've never worked with her, Seth says she's smart, and easy to work with. Why?"

"Along with Edward, Megan, Sparkey and now you, she is working with us to develop an announcement about Edward's retirement and Gregory's appointment as CFO. I agree she is smart. I'm going to call her and have her visit you later today. If anyone sees her, just say she is there to get information about the importance of our red yeast rice nutraceutical. You can trust her to keep the information under wraps. And I think you should be there to answer any of her questions."

"Yes. Call her. I'll have everything set up and waiting. I doubt if Victor will be around, but if he is, I'll confuse him by asking for funds to purchase some new piece of equipment." Shen smiled, picturing Victor's anger. "He will demand that I speak to him in his office. That should be enough of a cover to help Katherine search our records."

"Shen, she can't just arrive. Where would she begin and what would she look for?"

"If there is any problem at the facility, it would show up on our books. Since a review needs to be done anyway, it may turn something up. While I doubt we'll find anything, at least you will be able to narrow down your search within Marathon. Katherine isn't familiar with our end of the business, so by going over our accounts with me she may spot something I've missed."

"Doesn't Victor handle the accounts?"

"That bean counter? Sure, but I want to be sure that I haven't missed something. Anyway I can check to see if the lab needs supplies. As you know some of them have to be imported from Asia. Anyway, Victor wouldn't know dried Hawthorne berry from green tea."

Including Shen in his plan reassured Thomas. They had always worked well as a team. "It's too bad we couldn't just meet and enjoy lunch. It may be a long time between visits if I can't resolve this crisis quickly and quietly."

"I've been remiss as well. But when you get my report you will forgive my absence. You are right though, we must make time for friends.

19

Returning from her meeting with Mr. Sparks, Katherine was alerted by the ringing of her cell.

"Ms. Cunningham, this is Shen Lu. I was wondering if you would come out to the laboratory this afternoon. I would like to introduce you to our latest creation."

To say she was surprised to receive a call from the one senior executive that had intrigued her since joining the company, didn't begin to approach the truth. Never seen in New York headquarters, he was credited as the scientist behind Marathon Nutritionals most innovative products.

"Dr. Lu, this is an honor, and while I would love to visit, it has been a crazy day. I still need a little more than an hour to finish up a project."

"I can have a car meet you. If you leave by four o'clock, will that help? It really is important or I would schedule this for another day."

Checking her watch, and knowing that she had to reach the three reporters to set up the following day's interviews with Edward Abbott, Katherine decided yes, she could make the trip. After all, the lab was only an hour away, and she would still be home in time to get ready for Friday. "A car would be extremely helpful Dr. Lu. So, yes, have the driver meet me at four. I'll see you later."

Hanging up, Katherine took a deep breath. *No, this isn't convenient Dr. Lu. But then meeting you is an opportunity I can't resist.* Katherine had heard rumors of Dr. Lu's studying formulas in an old apothecary's recipe book. Even when working as a college intern, the scientist had kept so low a profile he was surrounded by mystery. Maybe she'd find out if the story about the ancient book was true? Adding to her delight was that Dr. Lu would be the only senior executive in the company that Charney might permit her to speak with. To Charney, her power was built on being the sole access to Marathon's top tier executives. The Chinese American scientist apparently wasn't included in Charney's restricted list of executives. *That's her loss,* Katherine thought.

I'd better check with Mr. Sweeney just in case. I want to be sure he knows that I will be going out to the Lab. Hearing her favorite George Strait tune, which signaled another call on her cell, she frowned. None of her friends would call during working hours.

"Katherine, its Thomas. I know you just spoke to Dr. Lu and I appreciate your agreeing to meet with him at his lab. He will explain everything. By the way, aren't you planning to speak to the reporters today? I'm sure things will go as you've planned. I have faith in you."

"Thank you for your support Thomas. I was just going to begin my calls."

"Don't forget to let me know if you have any questions. Call me anytime."

"Yes sir. I will." Hanging up, she released her breath, realizing that Dr. Lu wouldn't have called her before checking with Sweeney. Being trusted was a new feeling and she liked it. *Working for Thomas certainly makes me feel valued. What a change!*

Sinking further back into her desk chair, Katherine took a breath. OK. Now to the pitch. She hadn't pitched the media since college. Charney saw to that. Unlocking her credenza, she withdrew her tote bag into which she had placed a handwritten list of phone numbers for Sara Forman of CNN, Brian Harlin of *The Wall Street Journal, and* John Brawley of *Time*.

Katherine knew that Sara Forman had earned a reputation at CNN for tough reporting. Picking up her cell, she keyed in Sara's direct line. Fortunately she worked out of the New York Bureau and would hopefully be available. Breathing deeply, she whispered, "If interested."

Hearing a woman pick up and identify herself as Sara, she began, "Sara Forman, my name is Katherine Cunningham, I'm a vice president at Marathon Nutritionals and have something you might be interested in knowing about."

"Cunningham? I usually speak with a Sandra Charney."

"Well, yes, but Ms. Charney is out of town and this is a time-sensitive matter."

"You've got my attention, Ms. Cunningham"

"We are going to make an announcement tomorrow at 4 pm. I would like to offer you an exclusive television interview with one of our senior executives, but only on the promise that you will embargo the information until the announcement crosses the wire services."

"An exclusive? And who else will you be contacting? I doubt I'm your only fish."

"You are the only television journalist. There will be a similar offer made to a reporter at one newspaper and one news magazine." Sensing her hesitation, Katherine followed up a bit more slowly. "I will be happy to divulge their names once I have similar commitments from them. You are my first call."

"Are you really going to only offer three journalists access to this person?"

"Yes, I am. We haven't worked together, but I know your reputation for keeping an agreement. Do I have yours not to air your interview before tomorrow?"

"It will have to be a filmed, person-to-person interview."

"Agreed, but it will have to be set up in one of our conference rooms. And, Ms. Forman, I repeat, this is for tomorrow."

"OK. I'm in. I can have my crew there at noon. And I'll need at minimum fifteen minutes. Can you promise that?"

"Yes, Ms. Forman, I can. If you will confirm our arrangement in an email with the names of your crew later today, I will alert our Security Guards of your arrival."

"I'm looking forward to meeting you, Ms. Cunningham I appreciate your calling me with this TV exclusive."

"It is my pleasure. Till tomorrow."

Hanging up, Katherine reached for her cool plastic water bottle placing it on her forehead, then at the base of her neck. *One down, only two to go. She certainly does have an ego,* Katherine thought. *I guess only large egos make it on camera. Well, I don't have to worry about my ego. Charney keeps that in check daily.*

"Mr. Harlin, my name is Katherine Cunningham of Marathon Nutritionals. I'm calling to offer you an exclusive for *The Wall Street Journal.* It would be an interview with one of our senior executives concerning an announcement. But, as you are probably aware, the company is preparing itself for possible membership on NASDAQ, and we have to be very careful in the way we issue announcements."

"Are you telling me Marathon is going to list? Is that the announcement?"

"No sir, sorry, I didn't mean to mislead you. But the announcement is important to our company. I'm offering you the opportunity to be the only newspaper journalist to interview one of our senior executives. However..."

"'Isn't there always a 'however,' Ms. Cunningham? Go ahead. Hit me with it!"

"However, you will have to embargo the story until after 4 pm tomorrow at which time the announcement will have crossed the wires."

"And I can meet this person? Have a few minutes and something I can quote that is material to the company?"

"Yes, Mr. Harlin. Will you want me to set up the interview first thing in the morning?"

"I'm thinking three in the afternoon. It will make me think I'm actually writing for the wire and have a short deadline."

"Thank you, Mr. Harlin, not only for your interest, but for agreeing to my conditions. I will leave your name with our security guard for your 3 pm interview."

"You are welcome, Ms. Cunningham. We've never spoken, but I think I will like to work with you again. You say what you mean. Not the usual bull shit."

Laughing at his comment, she replied, "My pleasure in not sinking down to that level. Until tomorrow, Mr. Harlin." As she hung up, Katherine's hand lingered on the handset. *He is certainly light hearted on the phone. His interviews, however, are another story. Who knows, he may just be as nice as he seems.*

Checking her watch, Katherine saw that the two calls had only taken twelve minutes. Crossing her fingers that the third call would be as well received, she dialed John Brawley of *Time* magazine, one of the few news magazines still in print. Brawley was an old timer having earned his credentials in the days when New York City had six daily newspapers.

"Mr. Brawley…"

"Yeah?"

"I am sorry if I've interrupted something, but I think you will be interested in my call."

"Yeah?"

"Mr. Brawley, my name is Katherine Cunningham…"

"Cut to the chase. I haven't got all day, Miss."

"I am offering you an exclusive magazine interview with one of our senior executives concerning an announcement Marathon Nutritionals will be making tomorrow at 4 pm."

"Really? And why isn't that hard ass Charney calling me?"

"Ms. Charney is out of town. I'm empowered to offer you this opportunity if you agree to embargo your story until after 4 pm when the announcement is scheduled for release."

"Embargoed both online and in print?"

"Yes, Mr. Brawley. Are you interested?"

"I am if I can do it over the phone and if I can do it first thing in the morning. Around eight or eight-thirty."

"That can be arranged. If you give me your email address I will be happy to send you the number of a direct line for your call. Then if you require a photo or any additional information you will have my contact information."

"An exclusive you said? Not really."

"A magazine exclusive. I am contacting only three journalists of whom you are one. The others represent one television and one newspaper. Does that satisfy your requirements for exclusivity, Mr. Brawley? Do I have your word that you will keep to our embargo?"

"Yup. Tomorrow."

With her ear ringing from having the receiver slammed down at the end of the call, Katherine wiped the damp hand on her skirt. *What a curmudgeon! Now, if the heavens are aligned with earth they will each keep their promise and stick to reporting the facts."*

*   *   *

Alighting from the town car in front of Marathon Nutritionals' research facilities, Katherine stood still for a moment, looking at the low brick building with aged copper roof. It had always fascinated her that its exterior architecture from the 1880s was the antithesis of the ultra-modern and utilitarian interior.

Entering the building, she saw Dr. Lu walk towards her in welcome, waiting to usher her past security. "Ms. Cunningham, I can't tell you how I appreciate your fitting this visit into what I'm told is a stressful schedule."

"Fortunately, Dr. Lu, the Gods were working on my behalf today. You have my total attention."

Katherine preceded Dr. Lu, entering his spare but comfortable office set off to one side of the main laboratory. Looking around the Asian inspired room, she couldn't help commenting, "I love your office, Dr. Lu. It's a haven of serenity. Quite a change from headquarters."

"I knew I would like you Katherine. Outside of Thomas, no one I bring here thinks my taste is anything but eccentric."

"Your furnishings must be an inspiration as you work with your great grandfather's formulas." Was that smile confirmation the book existed? As she compared the office to the man, she thought, *you Dr. Lu, may have a Chinese office, but you dress like a metro sexual in that slim fitting suit.*

Settling in a chair across from Dr. Lu's desk, Katherine waited patiently. She had worked with the doctor's team over the years, each in a hurry to return to their labs, so she wasn't expecting Dr. Lu's cautious use of words. Nothing would seem to hurry him.

"Ms. Cunningham, Thomas has filled me in on the circumstances befalling Edward. I have known him since his first days with the company and find this incident to be as unacceptable as it is impossible to believe. I met with Thomas, and we thought that since you are part of a select circle working to clear up this predicament, you might do a little brainstorming with me as it pertains to this facility."

"Dr. Lu, I'm not a scientist. My only knowledge of your area is connected with writing your announcements. I don't see how I can help, though I truly want to be of assistance."

"You have a reporter's nose for a story. I want to go over our books with you and have you ask all the questions that may cross your mind. I'm hoping that between us this process will highlight an anomaly that can help us identify a rat."

"OK. Where do we start?"

"Let's move over to the work table. I've assembled several ledgers, but it may be easier to start working with a summary of this year's expenditures." As Katherine moved to the square wood table set in front of a window, she wondered how she would be any assistance. Numbers weren't her forte, words were.

"Katherine, we'll start at 'A' and work our way through the alphabet. I've printed out a general ledger summary listing each category of expenditure. When something occurs to you, I'll check it against our computerized records. That way, I can go back several years on any particular item, if necessary."

"'A' is a light listing. Let me see." As Katherine went down a list of ten items, the only one that seemed to catch her attention was Accessories. "Dr. Lu, Accessories? That seems to be a very general term. Can you break that down further?"

Walking back to his desk, he checked Accessories on his computer's records. "The breakdown shows several items all in the area of equipment. Each seems to be a small part, and in each case I recognize the items."

As they continued down the list and reached "C", Katherine learned that catering services were often required when a research project required 24-hour attention. Dr. Lu filled her in on some of the recent events that he had great hopes for adding to Marathon's line of nutraceuticals.

Then under "E" Katherine noticed a decrease in outlays for electricity. "Very good Katherine," Dr. Lu said. "A couple of years ago we installed several generators enabling the laboratory to maintain power during seasonal outages. New Jersey is still using above ground wires. During storms, downed wires can shut off our power. As you can imagine, loss of power would interrupt many of our 24-hour procedures."

Nearing the end of the alphabet and list of expenditures, Katherine was curious about an entry under the letter "V". "Dr. Lu, what are VC Services?"

Checking the listing on his computer screen, Dr. Lu, scratched his head turned to Katherine looking a bit surprised. "I believe they are a specialized cleaning company we hire to make sure the lab meets Occupational Safety and Health Administration's standards."

"How often do they come? Are you here? How long do they stay?"

"You know, I've never even seen one of their trucks. The building is cleaned regularly as are the New York offices, by a general cleaning crew. While we do contract out those services, most of the people have been here from the beginning. They arrive around 8 pm and leave around midnight three days a week."

"And VC Services?"

Checking his watch, Dr. Lu stood and offered Katherine his hand. He smiled. "Ms. Cunningham, you may have just identified a fly in the ointment. I wish this could wait, but you need to get back to your real responsibilities, and I must check something. May I take you to dinner when this is all over?"

"I'm pleased to have been some help. And, while it isn't necessary, I would enjoy dining with you. So thank you in advance."

*   *   *

No sooner had Katherine gotten into the limousine and Shen rushed back to his office. "Thomas," he almost yelled into the phone. "I think we have a lead. Can you give the following information to John Sparks and see if he can verify the location and headquarters of VC Services? I will email you the address, phone, and scan a copy of one of the company's invoices."

"Of course. Anything in particular you have in mind?"

"I believe it's a sham, possibly a shell company. Tell him to try to find out something about the company owners or size of its business. I will see if I can turn up anything of value here."

"On it. Thanks, Shen. This is the first solid bit of information we have to go on."

20

"OK, Thomas. I'll take a quick drive out to New Jersey. It's still early so I can at least get my eyes on this address."

Hanging up, Sparkey thoughts turned to Marathon. What did he actually know about the firm his friend founded more than two decades ago? Thinking back to their college days, Sparkey realized they knew each other's business lives pretty well. While neither was a specialist in the other's field, they had discussed their successes and failures over the years, during which they had become one another's mentor.

Sparkey called home and left a message for his wife saying he didn't know how late he would be and not to expect him. Jane usually had the answering machine on when she knew he'd be late

Looking at his watch, he realized he'd better hurry if he was going to hit this small town while people were still in diners or bars, both his favorite spots to gossip with the locals.

*　　　*　　　*

Parked on a side street of a small town that had been bypassed when the Interstate had been built, Sparkey dialed Thomas. "You aren't going to believe this. Did my photo come through?" he asked.

"Sparkey, all I can see is an empty lot. Even in the dark all I see is an open field of rubble."

"Yup. I'm going to do some scouting. I'll call you if I find anything." Hanging up, Sparkey drove on to the main street of one-story wood frame stores lining both sides of the road. The merchants included a dry cleaners, bakery, grocery/deli shop, Laundromat, bar, and liquor store.

At the end of the street stood the local diner, not much different from the other storefronts in town. Sparkey could see into the brightly lit restaurant noting the usual counter, table and booth seating arrangements. Parking in a lot off to one side of the building, he approached the front door on alert for someone to engage in conversation. If he was lucky it would be a woman only too willing to talk to a stranger. And hopefully, that someone would have a surprising tidbit related to his case. That was one of the things he loved about his job talking to people from all walks of life.

Settling onto a counter stool, Sparkey smiled at the approaching waitress.

"What'll you have?" Her name tag read Lizzie. She was short, plump and he guessed her to be in her mid-forties. Her thick Jersey accent pegged her as a local. In his younger days, before falling for Jane, he might have been interested in seeing how friendly she was. When on the trail of some elusive character, a pleasing female could ease his loneliness. No longer, Jane had taken away that empty feeling with her love.

"A menu and coffee. This looks like a nice place. What's your specialty?" His smile lingered and was rewarded with a nod. Apparently Lizzie wasn't into conversation.

As the waitress poured his coffee, Sparkey turned to the side, giving the customers a quick once over. Swinging back around he gave Lizzy one of his best smiles. "So what's a nice girl like you doing in this place?"

Her laughter was the kind that stayed inside more like a comment. Friendly, but cautious. Still holding the coffee pot, she gave him a knowing look while placing a set of flatware wrapped in a paper napkin in front of him. "Our fish and chips are a local favorite. The fish is fresh from the ocean this morning. Some like our steak n' fries. Everyone likes our apple pie."

"OK, Lizzie. I'll have your steak n' fries, and apple pie for dessert."

After shouting to the chef in the pass through window to the kitchen, Lizzie turned back. "My dad owns this place. I've been here all my life." Smiling a bit more warmly, she seemed in no hurry to step away.

"Then you know just about everyone and everything that goes on here."

"I guess so. And what is a handsome, married stranger like you wanting to know about our little town?"

"Oh, Lizzie, I think I love you. Smart, friendly, and happy to talk to a traveler." No sooner had Sparkey taken his second sip of a very good cup of coffee, Lizzie slapped a plate down in front of him. It was filled to the rim with a slab of meat and crispy fries, and no attempt had been made to make it neat or attractive. Not wanting to seem in a hurry he took a first bite of the surprisingly tender piece of beef, and as he slowly chewed, he gave Lizzie a smile of appreciation.

While Sparkey ate, he tuned into the conversations around him. One couple was worried about meeting the month's mortgage payment. "Ann Marie, we have to find a way to get your boss to give you more hours. I'm due for a raise, now I'll have to ask for it. Who knows, with business as bad as it is, he may cut my salary instead."

A couple in their twenties, were more interested in each other than the burgers on their plates. Then there was a man in his late sixties, grey all over from his sparse hair to his shirt and slacks, sitting off by himself with a book. He looked like he'd been planted there as part of the décor.

Sparkey's ears perked up as two men entered the diner and were settling into a booth directly behind him. They were so intent on their conversation, they weren't aware of being overheard. At the mention of the street behind the diner, the street which included VC Services' business address, Sparkey had all he could do to swallow his last bite of steak.

"We already own half of the block but we need the rest before we can interest a national food chain in the property. It was lucky to have found that first seller. He said he was planning on using it for his business and needed the lot large enough for a commercial garage. But you know, he was a bit too slick. That guy never had grease under his fingernails."

"No matter, we got the property at a good price. Now with luck, we can get the rest. This town is dying. People are old and willing to sell. We just have to be patient."

And so Sparkey guessed that VC Services never had a business in this town or any other. Finishing his pie, he paid his check and left a 30% tip for Lizzie. *There you go sweetheart. For your smile and customers.*

"Thanks, traveler. Do stop this way again." Lizzie's smile was the real deal and Sparkey gave her a salute as he turned and left the cozy little restaurant.

*   *   *

Back at his office Sparkey booted up his computer. A search found a VC Services registered in Delaware as an environmental specialist in cleaning laboratories and food service establishments. The information was sketchy. The address was the same he had visited. The New Jersey lot was registered to a Mr. Charles. There was no information on either number of employees or company value. The reality was that practically anyone could register a company in Delaware with only a driver's license as proof of identity.

Very interesting, Sparkey thought. *This is getting a bit too neat. VC Services with a Marathon customer and Mr. Charles its owner. A shell company to do what?* Picking up his phone he called Thomas.

"Thomas. Tell Shen I think the rat is Victor. He may not be the blackmailer, but if this company's a sham, Victor would be the logical suspect. He'd have to not only register a legitimate company, create a fictitious location like the one I just visited, but go through normal Marathon Nutritionals security protocols before VC Services would be vetted to work for the company."

"Why would Victor be the only one with that capability? Couldn't one of our business contacts know enough to tackle a scam of this kind? Even perpetrate similar scams with other companies?" Thomas asked.

"Other than Shen, Victor is the only other executive who would authorize hiring a service to clean the lab. But we need proof. First, can you replace the money before tomorrow's announcement…oops, that's later today. I had to call. I just wasn't aware it was midnight."

"Not to worry. Yes, the money will be back in the Foundation's account tomorrow morning. As for proof. What do you need?"

"In my experience the embezzler always has an accomplice. If that is what Victor has been up to with VC Services, we need to identify that person. Additionally, there are usually records. A paper trail. I'm hoping that by checking into your company's financial records, we may dig something up. I want to do a cursory audit of anything Victor may be involved with. Can you give me access to those files?"

"Not directly and, not without Victor hearing about it. What did you think of Katherine?"

"Do I detect something my friend? A glimmer of interest maybe?"

"Who knows? But for now, I'm asking what you think of the young woman?" Thomas answered.

"I liked her and she has agreed to try to help me if possible."

"Good. She practically lives in our file room. Can this wait until Saturday? She is going to be busy with the announcement and its aftermath. Probably up to 7 pm at least."

"Would she be willing to stay late and work with me via cell phone? In that way I can direct her search for that crucial bit of evidence that may expose Victor's double-dealing. However, I still haven't linked him to that video, and to Edward. He may be an embezzler, but blackmail? I'm hoping Jake can find some connection. If he does, then our little accountant is a dangerously twisted man."

"Did Katherine give you her contact information?"

"Yes."

"Then why not call her now? That way, if she agrees to work with you, she can schedule her day to include your search."

"It's midnight!"

"She's a trooper. Katherine will understand the urgency. Sandra returns from vacation tomorrow evening, so she's probably going be happy to help you sooner rather than later."

"By the way, how does she get along with the Dragon Lady?" Sparkey asked.

"She's smart and has kept to Sandra's rules. It's my guess that Katherine is the backbone of that department. What is that saying? 'Anyone who controls the information is in control?' I doubt she thinks of herself that way. My guess is Sandra's well aware of Katherine's importance to the department."

"OK. I'll keep you posted." Hanging up, Sparkey wondered how Katherine worked with Sandra Charney. The woman had a problem with other women, especially when they were younger. He'd first spotted it when he brought his wife to a company function. Jane was a stunning redheaded Irish lass he'd met in Dublin. They fell madly in love, and Jane had followed him home. Ten years later she was still a stunner.

Dialing Katherine's home number, Sparkey made a list of the files he hoped would reveal more about VC Services. "Katherine, I'm sorry if I woke you." Sparkey heard a clear voice. It didn't sound like someone he'd woken from a deep sleep even if it was midnight.

"I'm not sleeping, Mr. Sparks. Too much running around in my mind to even think of falling asleep. What can I do for you?"

"I know that tomorrow is a big day. The Marathon Nutritionals' announcement is scheduled for release, and prior to that, you will be overseeing reporters interviewing Edward."

Sparkey heard her sigh. "I am sorry to add to your day, but it's crucial. Would you stay at the end of it and help me do some sleuthing? It may take a couple of hours. I can't be seen at the company, so we'll stay in touch by cell phone. Will you help me?" Sparkey was pacing around the office. He had to get into the files. Katherine seemed willing to help. Could she find the files he needed?

"Yes, Mr. Sparks, I'll help you. But what am I looking for? Where do you think I'll find it?"

"In the file room. I understand that's a place you are very familiar with."

Chuckling, Katherine replied, "You might say it's my personal office, Mr. Sparks. I'll call you when the coast is clear and I am in the file room."

"Thanks Katherine, I'm counting on you."

21

With little sleep, Katherine arrived at her office and booted up her laptop. Her mind focused on the day of interviews, a day that would either make or break any chances to advance her career. Opening Sara's email, she saw the names of the CNN film crew and noticed the addition of a makeup artist. Printing Sara's names and that of *Wall Street Journal's* Brian Harlin on the building's security form, along with arrival times and her extension, she whispered, "Signed, sealed, now to deliver." She got on the elevator and hit the button for the lobby floor.

Once she spotted Joseph at the security desk, she was reassured. He wouldn't send anyone up to the executive floor without contacting her first. "Hi Joe, it is going to be a busy day for me. Here is a list of my guests. Please call me before you let them pass."

"Sure thing, Ms. Cunningham. We haven't seen much of you lately. They must be keeping you busy?"

"No busier than usual. Today is different. I want to be ready to meet each of these people at the elevator. Take care, and thank you, Joe."

No sooner had she returned to her office she found Mr. and Mrs. Abbott waiting. Both wore tailored business suits, appeared composed, and were silent. "Good morning. Are you both ready for a stressful day?"

"As ready as I can be." Edward Abbott replied, reaching out to take his wife's hand.

"Why don't you both try to relax and I'll get us some coffee," Megan said rising slowly from her chair. "Katherine, I believe you take yours black?"

She was pleased by Megan's offer. Katherine had liked Megan all those years ago. She practically ran Mr. Rosso's department and subtly kept Katherine out of the dictator's range of fire. "Thank you, Mrs. Abbott. I think we had better go up to the executive conference room. I have asked that it be setup with coffee and a selection of pastries. We can wait there."

"Katherine, its Megan, to people I like."

Smiling as she remembered why she had liked this woman, she nodded. "Megan."

Entering the executive conference room, Megan moved away from her husband and over to the sideboard, returning with coffee and a Danish for her husband and Katherine. Both were standing inside the long room, silently involved with their own thoughts. "Katherine, I'll just sit off to the side so you and Edward will have the table to yourselves." As she walked away Katherine noticed that Megan Abbott had selected a chair out of her husband's line of sight.

Yes, her PR background had prepared her for today. Megan Abbott understood that Katherine had to be the one he looked to for direction.

Taking a seat next to Edward, Katherine studied his controlled calm. She leaned over and whispered, "You are a lucky man, Mr. Abbott. You have a woman who is both lovely and smart for a wife." Watching him relax a bit, she realized that this was a love affair she envied. Here was a man in trouble and wife standing at the ready to help him recover his self-worth, not to mention his reputation. A reputation that someone wanted to trash.

"Are you ready for the telephone call from *Time* Magazine's reporter, John Brawley? I must warn you he's tough old school, more Damon Runyon than Tom Brokaw."

"I've been reading those clips you sent over. And I think I've met him at one of the corporate meetings." The phone rang, and Katherine answered it on the speaker phone.

"I'm a bit early, Ms. Cunningham, but my day is packed. Can we get this over with now?" The gruff voice had both of them sitting taller in their chairs.

"Absolutely, Mr. Brawley. Mr. Abbott is here, so you can direct your questions to him."

"Mr. Abbott, what's this announcement about?"

"At 4 pm today, Marathon Nutritionals will announce my resignation and the promotion of Gregory Pomeroy to Chief Financial Officer."

"Why? You're still a young man."

"I've been told to cut the stress in my life for health reasons. I don't want to become an invalid before I grow old."

"But word on the street is that Marathon is planning to go public. Why would you leave before seeing that corporate milestone through to completion? It could represent a great deal of money for you personally."

"You may quote me, Mr. Brawley. Gregory will be the perfect officer to handle all of the reports and filings necessary when Marathon Nutritionals prepares its public offering. It is best for the company that he be in position prior to implementation of a strategy as important as this will be to the company's future. As for wealth, I can't spend it if I'm dead."

Katherine had wondered how he would cut Brawley short. Mentioning his possible death certainly was final.

"That it would. One more thing, is Gregory Pomeroy qualified…as qualified as you have been?"

"Thank you for your vote of confidence, Mr. Brawley. Yes, Gregory has been my assistant long enough that he can complete my sentences. I hope I've answered all your questions."

"Yup. I'll run a paragraph on the 6 pm online edition. If I need anything more early next week when I write my piece for the magazine, I'll call you."

"No, please direct your inquiries to Ms. Cunningham. If necessary she can reach me, and I'll get back to you promptly."

"Right. I guess we're through. Bye Abbott."

Katherine looked away when Megan walked to her husband and gave him a solid kiss on his mouth.

"Well done, Mr. Abbott. Its only 8:15 you're free until 11:30. Sara Forman will be bringing a makeup artist to touch you up for the CNN filmed one-on-one. I realize she said noon. But I have a feeling she'll be early."

* * *

Katherine wasn't getting much done, worried that Sara would pull a fast one. She didn't get her anchor's position by being soft on her subjects. Sitting at the conference room table and reviewing her list of possible questions, she realized she'd have to rely on her gut to evade any problems raised by this seasoned broadcaster.

She had been right. At 11:30 the security guard called to announce the arrival of Sara and her CNN crew. Instructing the guard to wait five minutes before directing them to the executive elevator bank, Katherine phoned Abbott's office where he and his wife had been waiting. "Mr. Abbot, CNN is here. I'll settle them in Conference Room A and then come and get you."

When Katherine reached the doors to the elevator, she planted a smile on her face. "Good morning, Ms. Forman, I'm Katherine Cunningham. Please follow me." As she led the small group to the main executive conference room, she heard the men commenting on the lack of glitzy furnishings. Smiling to herself, she hoped this would engender a kinder reception of Abbott and the company. Lately, reporters seemed ready to take a poke at any organization that exhibited signs of pretentious wealth. *At least they won't find any gold bathroom fixtures*, she thought. All paintings and furnishings were tailored, traditional office design.

"There is coffee on the sideboard. Please help yourselves. I'll get Mr. Abbott for you Ms. Forman. I won't be but a minute." *Please let her questions be brief, not rambling thoughts hoping to trap Edward in a lengthy response.*

Katherine returned to the group. "Mr. Abbott may I introduce Sara Forman, CNN's 6 pm New York Bureau news anchor."

Sara quickly maneuvered Edward to a chair so the makeup artist could prep him for the camera. She certainly wasn't in to small talk, as the trim woman then began directing the film crew to where she wanted to be seated for the interview.

"Ms. Cunningham, I think we can do this in about fifteen minutes. Will that be all right?"

"Ms. Forman, we have set aside twenty minutes. Please let me know if you will need any support material at the end of your interview and I will arrange to have it sent over."

Knowing that a filmed interview would be the most uncomfortable for Edward, she poured two glasses of water making sure she had a napkin alongside his glass. Stepping back out of camera range, Katherine waited for Sara Forman to begin. *Ms. Anchor looks cool unlike her reputation for having a temper.* Crossing her fingers, Katherine waited and prayed Edward wouldn't stumble. Film was dangerous for the inexperienced, doubly so if the interviewer was after blood.

"You are a surprise, Mr. Abbott. I believe Sandra Charney makes all official announcements. I'm intrigued. And, I must say, delighted to be sitting here in the executive offices of Marathon Nutritionals headquarters."

"Yes. Ms. Charney is Marathon's spokesperson. However, this announcement is personal to me."

"Oh? And what is this announcement that has the company's CFO available for our interview?"

"At 4 pm today, Marathon will be announcing my retirement and that Gregory Pomeroy will be the new CFO of the corporation."

"What? This is a surprise. I've attended your corporate meetings and you were the go to person regarding the company's financials. Is Mr. Pomeroy qualified to fill your ample shoes?"

"You flatter me, Ms. Forman. Yes, Mr. Pomeroy has been my assistant for several years. I have complete faith that he will carry out his duties admirably."

"Mr. Abbott, you parallel the growth of the company. My question is why are you retiring?"

"During a routine doctor's visit, I realized the stress of my job was causing me some minor health problems.

That if I reduced this stress while relatively young, I can live to be an old man."

"Marathon Nutritionals is rumored to be introducing a new nutraceutical. Is this true? Can you tell me anything about it?"

"My field is financial. However, to answer your question, Dr. Lu has just completed testing on a new product with an efficacy dating back thousands of years."

"You've got my attention. Go on."

"Well our company believes that there are many ancient formulations that have never been tested using modern scientific protocols. Among these formulas are some natural ingredients with a more moderate approach to treating specific symptoms and conditions. Marathon Nutritionals as you know is not a pharmaceutical company. We do not make drugs. What we manufacture are natural ingredients to supplement a person's diet. And the upcoming introduction is one we are very excited about." Holding up his hand, palm facing the extremely attentive reporter, he continued. "I am afraid that is all I can say at the moment."

Settling back in her chair, Sara, continued in her business-like manner. "Have you been thinking about retiring for a while? If so, what do you plan to do?"

"No, this decision is a recent one. As for my future, I may work with outreach groups treating childhood diseases in this country's poorer communities. My plans aren't as yet defined. First, I have to finish bringing Mr. Pomeroy up-to-speed on current projects."

"Then?"

Smiling and in softer voice, Edward replied, "And then I'm going to take my wife on a long trip."

"I'd be remiss if I didn't ask why you aren't lightening your workload instead of retiring."

Focusing squarely on the brash woman, Edward Abbott replied, "I just answered that question, Sara. It is the perfect time for a transition of this importance. The company is on solid footing. It has several important products in its pipeline and when, and if, it does begin activities towards becoming a public company, there should be a steady CFO at the helm."

Katherine didn't realize she had been holding her breath. But Edward Abbott had fielded the trick question as smoothly as if she had written it. *Why was I even worried he could handle this woman?* She wondered.

"Is there anything else, Ms. Forman? I believe your interview has all the pertinent information?"

Rising and shaking Edward Abbott's hand, Sara Forman looked over to Katherine. "We're done for now. If I could have a copy of both Mr. Abbott and Mr. Pomeroy's history with the company that will help me fill out my story."

"I'll see that they are emailed to you shortly." Walking to the door and opening it for Sara and her crew, Katherine was relieved the woman hadn't tried to button hole her into adding any additional information. She had enough to cut into sound bites of a few seconds each.

"Well done, Edward. You didn't give her anything extra to use against the company. Let's hope your last interview of the day goes as smoothly. Why don't we reconvene here at 2:45, just in case the *Wall Street Journal* reporter also arrives early?"

It was 1:45 by the time Katherine returned to her office. Calling down to a nearby deli, she ordered a chicken salad sandwich and coffee. While she waited, she sent bios of both Edward Abbott and Gregory Pomeroy to Sara as promised. Was this too easy? Would the *WSJ* reporter throw Edward a bombshell? All she could do was be alert for any unpleasant surprises.

As she ate her sandwich, Katherine hoped that after this last interview Mr. and Mrs. Abbott could relax. She, on the other hand would be on tender hooks until 4 pm, then monitoring the news until early evening. People not in public relations thought that simply getting the interview was the end of her job. It was only the beginning. She had to stay on top of the press, just in case a reporter got the information wrong or stated something glaringly untrue. Her job then was to get either a retraction or correction to clarify the company's position.

*   *   *

Brian Harlin was a surprise. The trimly dressed man wearing a blazer, slacks and open collar blue shirt walked leisurely towards her. He looked to be about forty, more of a country club casual than a British financier in tailored suit and braces. With a warm smile that melted her reserve, Katherine wondered if she was meeting a wolf in sheep's clothing.

"Ms. Cunningham, may I call you Katherine?" Stepping forward and taking her extended hand, the attractive man wrapped it in both of his and squeezed just enough to be more than polite. *Mm, what was that two-handed shake? Flirting?*

"Of course, Brian. Please do. I am looking forward to your interview with Mr. Abbott and will be available later if you require additional information. Please follow me." Leading this charmer to the conference room, she excused herself to get Edward. *Too bad this is work. That is one man I would love to go out with. All male, sexy smile and showing interest in me.*

Stepping into the office Edward and Megan had been using, Katherine's mind refocused on the interview. "Mr. Abbott I have to warn you that while Brian Harlin seems to be an open and charming pro, he is a pro with the *Wall Street Journal.* I'm just reminding you to keep to the script with your usually brief responses."

Edward Abbott didn't appear as calm as he had been for either *Time* or CNN, she knew he had studied Harlan's hard hitting articles and saw potential for danger. As a private company Marathon was not required to release its financials. Would Edward Abbott be tricked into disclosing sensitive company information?

Standing as they entered the conference room, Brian Harlin held out his hand, "Mr. Abbott, I don't know if you remember me, but I was the reporter who asked for specific financial forecasts during your last corporate meeting."

Edward looked the somewhat taller man in the eye, shook his hand and smiled. "Brian, yes, I remember only too clearly. I also remember you didn't embroider your column with anything less than the truth. So I am pleased you are here to listen to what I have to say."

Hell. They look like two friends settling in for a social chat. Katherine could only hope Brian was going to listen to Edward and didn't have another agenda.

"Ok what is this announcement I've agreed not to release until it crosses the wires at four today?"

As Edward gave the brief overview of his retirement and Gregory Pomeroy's promotion, she noticed that Brian had taken only a few notes on a very small notepad. Usually, a reporter would ask to tape a conversation. Not this one.

"Is there some difficulty with Marathon? A reason you chose to retire at such a young age?"

"No, Brian, not with the company. With my health." Raising his hand to ward off a question about details, Edward continued. "I was recently diagnosed with hypertension. It runs in my family. As you know the company has grown into a vast complex requiring more and more of my attention. I realized that if we go public, that will only be compounded. Since I want to live to an old age, this would seem to be the best time to make a change."

"That's all? A minor condition? Not a dire disease?"

"It's as simple as that." Edward replied looking like he knew Brian's question had been a trap. "Of course it is an important announcement for the company. Our business associates and customers want to be assured that Marathon is being managed by qualified leadership. That is why I wanted to be the spokesperson about my own retirement."

Katherine watched as Edward leaned back in his chair and crossed his legs. *Am I imaging it, or is he enjoying this interview?* She mused.

"You aren't required to share your numbers with me. Can you share something that will be of interest to my readers about the impact of your resignation on the company? They will want to be satisfied that your retirement isn't due to your being involved in anything criminal or that you are being investigated for leaking company secrets."

"You are right, Brian. Your readers would appreciate my telling you if I was involved in anything nefarious. Since I can't, they would appreciate knowing that Marathon is experiencing a dramatic period of growth. We are part of a $23 billion dollar industry. And Marathon, due primarily to consumer acceptance of our philosophy of providing innovative products, has doubled its retail accounts in the past eighteen months. As we continue to develop new products to resolve nutritional deficiencies, we look forward to continuing on this trajectory of growth. The only management change is mine. Gregory Pomeroy has been an inspired assistant who is more than capable of replacing me as CFO."

Hell, anything nefarious? Had Brian heard something? Is there a leak about Edward Abbott's difficulties? Katherine couldn't sit still, crossing her hands that moments before had been lying quietly in her lap. For now it was out of her hands. There was nothing she could do but wait and see where Brian went next. Silently she prayed, *Edward, listen to every word Brian says. Take your time before answering.*

Turning the page of his notepad, the crafty reporter launched right in to his next question. His change in posture alerted Katherine to a possible curve ball. "As you know, the public is somewhat mistrustful of corporations. They believe that as a group they are only interested in profits, not in the security or advancement of their employees. My readers would like to know if Marathon is different."

What had she expected, a powder puff interview? Crossing her fingers, Katherine waited for Edward's response.

"I'm not prepared to provide you with our human resources policies, Brian. However, it might interest your readers to know that more than 80% of our employees either moved East with the company, or have been with us since relocating to the New York area. I would expect that to be a very favorable reputation in any industry."

"You have sidestepped me expertly, Mr. Abbott. I believe my time is up. I will be happy to print your announcement as issued, and may add a few of your comments to humanize the story. Thank you for your time."

Rising, the two men shook hands. Katherine also reached out to shake the reporter's hand. "Brian, here is my business card. Should you think of anything else, please call me."

Standing a bit nearer than he would if talking with a man, Brain gave her a dreamy look that she was sure had melted many a female's reserve. "Well, I'm just in time to write the story, and file it for tomorrow's edition." He continued in a voice soft enough to only be heard by her. "I don't have to turn the story in until 4:20."

Katherine relaxed. "Good bye, Brian. It has been refreshing."

"May I call you and not Ms. Charney in the future? I'd much prefer working with you."

Is he kidding? "Anytime. I'd be happy to take you calls." In all her years in business she'd met two kinds of men. Those who genuinely enjoyed women and those who used them as accessories to their lives. Here was a full-blooded member of the group who liked to flirt. What she wanted to do was flirt back. *Oh well, maybe in a next life. Then again, why can't I mix business with pleasure?*

Once Brian had left, Katherine remembered Alice and her promise to drop off the information she had prepared for her difficult boss. Well no time like the present. Thanking Mr. and Mrs. Abbott for their forbearance, she rushed back to her office where she picked up the envelope, hoping she wouldn't be waylaid. She had to get back to her office before four so she could monitor the announcement coverage by the various news feeds.

Approaching Alice's outer office, Katherine knocked before walking to the woman's desk. "As promised. I appreciate your seeing that Ms. Charney has the information on time." Katherine turned and left without waiting for a response.

Promptly at 4 pm, the automated system released the Marathon Nutritionals' announcement to the Dow Jones, AP, Reuters, and Bloomberg news bureaus.

Checking her Bloomberg terminal as it reported the announcement's coverage, Katherine read each item carefully trying to identify mistakes or unexpected information. Next she checked *Time*, CNN, and *WSJ* to make sure that the reporters had kept their promise not to release the information before it was disseminated by the wire services. She was greatly relieved that they had. The Bloomberg terminal was a godsend as it enabled her to monitor all news relevant to Marathon Nutritionals, from not only news sources but the investment community.

Katherine quickly sent personal thank you notes to each reporter. It was important to her that each be made to feel that Marathon appreciated their interest and accuracy of their reports. Her note to Brian was warmer than the rest, implying that she was pleased by his succinct and accurate coverage, without letting on that she was aware it hadn't been the story he wanted to write. *Well he's let us off the hook for now.* She suspected he would be shadowing every action Marathon took in the near future and at the first hint of problems, would be calling her for verification.

By 6:30 all sources, those expected and some unexpected, had printed the information without mistakes or embellishment. For the moment, her job was done.

22

Katherine was traveling the back stairs from her office floor up to the file room. Fortunately the stairwell was illuminated by emergency lighting installed after 9/11. She remembered the stories of people being trapped in their offices for up to seven hours, waiting for the fire department to lead them though pitch black hallways and stairwells with their emergency lanterns and flash lights. After that threat the building had installed lighting systems that would engage when sensors detected someone in the area. In that way employees would have continual illumination, especially in the event of a power failure.

As Katherine approached the main entrance of the file room, she felt she was trespassing. Which was of course silly, since the file room was her second home, a place she spent most of her working life. But her normal hours spent in the room with row upon row of steel file cabinets were during the late morning, not in early evening.

Using her key card, she entered the file room and turned on the lights. Even though it was after seven

Katherine wanted to avoid unexpected company so she secured the door's dead bolt behind her. She took out her cell and hit John Sparks' number, hoping he was standing by. She didn't relish being alone in the building any later than necessary.

"Mr. Sparks, I'm in the file room. Where do you want me to start? And what am I looking for?" she asked after he answered.

"Katherine I know all company records are backed up on computer. What I'm looking for are hand written notes, even signatures."

"I'm ready, give me the specifics."

"Go to the accounts payable files. I don't know how they're set up. Let me know if they are kept by department or, filed in a separate accounting department location."

As she walked through aisles of file cabinets five feet high, Katherine remembered having to search for an invoice for Sandra Charney. Her boss had wanted to see a printing bill that she was sure had been inflated beyond the originally contracted amount. That was when she found that all accounts payable and receivable records were kept under lock and key in a separate section of the room. As she glanced over the rows of steel cabinets she spotted her target in the last row against the back wall of the room. With her set of office keys in hand, she selected the one that gave her access to everything in the room.

"OK, John, I am in the accounting department's file cabinet. The files are set up alphabetically by department, with each business in its own folder, and the most recent invoices placed first."

"Katherine is there a folder for VC Services? If so, open it and see who authorized payment."

"I've got it. It looks like all the invoices have been signed by Mary Johnson. That's Mr. Rosso's assistant."

"Is there a cancelled check?"

"A copy, not the original. Mary's signature is on the company's stamp. The bank is the First Commerce Bank of Delaware."

"Katherine, take a photo of the stamp with Mary's signature and the check, both front and back, and send them to me. Now I need you to find the employment reimbursement files. I'm looking for Victor Rosso's expense folder."

"Just a minute." Having emailed the photos from her cell she headed to a nearby cabinet and pulling out Rosso's folder wondered what Mr. Sparks was hoping to find. "Found."

"Is there any banking or credit card information? Maybe he reimbursed the company for something? A trip, luncheon, something like that."

"I see that he reimbursed the company for a trip to Andorra last year. It was an American Express card invoice for air travel. I'll photo that as well. It looks like Mr. Rosso doesn't travel much. There are no other travel related charges in his file. Other expenses relate to business publications and entertaining company suppliers."

"Were there any charges relating to Andorra on that American Express invoice? Maybe a hotel or restaurant? And is there a copy of the airline ticket?"

"No ticket, just a copy of the American Express invoice with airline ticket charge."

"Interesting. OK, send me a copy of that charge. Now, is Victor's resume or employment history available? It's probably in the human resources section."

"Are you sure we should be checking into Mr. Rosso's personnel records?"

"I have Mr. Sweeney's permission to go where ever necessary. Katherine I am sure you understand how critical this search is to uncovering Edward Abbott's blackmailer."

"Right. I had to ask. OK, I'm in HR's section. Nine years ago they interviewed Victor Charles Rosso. The interviewer's comments are attached to his employment record along with his resume. Interesting, his previous employment history is only mentioned in general. No employer or references are listed. I'm sending photos of these now."

"I've just given your photos a once over and they're crisp. I think we have all we need for the present. Thank you, Katherine. These records are invaluable. I may call you tomorrow if I need to verify anything else."

"If you do need me, I'll be at home."

"No problem. Really, this is very helpful. Good night, Katherine."

"Good bye." Katherine hoped it was good bye. She wasn't comfortable checking into anyone's personnel files, especially not a senior executive's. She didn't know how Mr. Rosso was involved. While she remembered not liking him, her main dislike had to do with his having the personality of a prima donna. Maybe Mr. Sparks is just cross checking information to rule Rosso out?

23

Wheeling her oversized suitcase into the lobby of her upper eastside apartment building, Sandra nodded to the doorman and headed straight toward the concierge's desk. "Good evening, George. Do you have anything for me?"

"Yes, Ms. Charney. Your mail and an envelope that just arrived by messenger. Welcome home."

She accepted the pile of paper, and checked the return address on the messengered envelope. Satisfied that it was from Cunningham, Sandra headed for the elevator pulling her suitcase while balancing a large tote bag in one hand and her foot-high stack of mail in the other. Once inside she punched the 20th floor button with her elbow. "Almost home," she whispered. While Ian had been a delightful interlude, what she needed now was to be cosseted in her own surroundings with no one to disturb her solitude.

The pleasure she felt upon opening the door to her apartment never failed. This was her safe haven. Turning to close and double lock her door, she released the handle of her suitcase, unloaded her mail and tote bag on a small table, and stood facing her living room alight with the glow of late afternoon sun. A feeling of peace enveloped her as she viewed the treasures she'd accumulated over the years. A portrait painted of her by a brief, long ago lover had preserved her twenties for all time. A silver mirror said to have been in the home of one of the Biltmore's was purchased with her first bonus check. The custom furnishings had been commissioned one by one, and the prized crystal accessories were purchased when she needed a pat on the back for surviving yet another crisis of confidence. Her flawless home was the reward for a life of extraordinary discipline.

From her very first studio apartment, she had set about duplicating a photo she'd seen in an interior decorator's magazine she'd found in her high school library. Her mother certainly didn't know anything about style in either home décor or fashionable clothes. To her mother a harmoniously furnished home was a waste of money that she needed for booze. Sandra had been lucky to have a new bed spread covering her third-hand mattress.

Breathing in the light scent of furniture polish left behind by her cleaning woman, she surveyed her living room and thought back to her very first apartment when she'd been a night school student at City University. She'd furnished it with hard earned dollars waitressing the 6 am to 4 pm shift at a neighborhood diner. One of the first purchases had been a wooden deck chair she'd often fallen asleep on when studying for exams. Now the chair was a counterpoint to more expensive pieces, some she had lovingly purchased at auction. But she'd kept that spare wooden chair as a reminder of just how far she had come, from a small town in Upstate New York to the Upper Eastside of Manhattan. Everything she was today was due to her own efforts. She had learned from an early age that she had only herself to rely on.

The room's anchor was a deep red and black modern designed carpet centered on her living room floor. On two edges of the carpet sat pristine white sofas set at right angles with not a wrinkle to mar their soft cushions. Two deep chairs upholstered in a rich red tapestry were placed opposite the sofas with a square black lacquer coffee table positioned in between. The fabric she'd chosen for her upholstered chairs was repeated in the tailored valance and window drapes. Her pride and joy was a large cut crystal vase filled with glass marbles awaiting a fresh bunch of lilies. It had been given to her by a long ago man she'd entertained as a possible husband. Of course marriage was out of the question when she had learned that the duplicitous bastard had been married. "My wife and I don't live together. But she is so wonderful with the kids. We have an understanding," he had explained. But she had loved him, and the crystal perfection remained a reminder of a love that couldn't be.

There were no family photographs in silver frames, no books displayed on the large coffee table, in fact not one book in sight. Sandra Charney wasn't aware of any deficiency in her decorating. Books and photos belonged in another magazine photo, the one with a family. A mother, father, and two children, one boy and one girl. So perfect, she remembered thinking all those years ago, somehow knowing at age fourteen that life wouldn't be hers.

No sooner had she taken in the beauty of her orderly home the silence was shattered by the ringing of her phone. "Hello?"

"Welcome back Sandra. It's Thomas. I wanted to give you a heads up on an announcement that crossed the wires at 4 pm today."

Sandra felt her hand grip the phone as if to crush it; her pleasurable mood replaced by a nagging fear. "I'll stop by the office and help with the media, Thomas. I can be there in fifteen minutes."

"No need. I've enlisted Ms. Cunningham for this project, and so far her planning and execution of this small announcement have been quite satisfactory. In fact, I want to ask you to direct any calls from reporters concerning this to her attention."

"And, this announcement…what was it about?" Sandra hoped the ice in her veins wasn't being transmitted by her voice.

"Oh, simply that Edward has retired and Gregory has been named as his replacement. I wanted to make sure we got as little attention as possible and it couldn't wait for your return. I'm sure you understand."

"Very little, attention? That isn't usually the way we handle management changes at Mr. Abbott's level."

"No. But this time that is what I wanted. Oh, one other thing, I will need Ms. Cunningham for another small project that should take most of this coming week. I will need her full attention."

By now Sandra's entire body was rigid. "I'll make sure not to bother Ms. Cunningham until I hear from you. Thomas is there anything I may do to facilitate this new project? You seem to have been undertaking a number of communications activities in my absence."

"That's very kind of you Sandra. I think you know I consider you an extremely valuable member of my executive team. So my borrowing Ms. Cunningham should free you for more serious undertakings. I'm very glad to have found you at home. But you must be tired after your trip, so I'll say good night."

"Good night, Thomas. Please call if I may help in any way." Hitting the off button on her cordless phone, Sandra stood rooted to the floor, the receiver still griped in her hand, her mind a blank. Only a roaring in her ears brought her partially out of shock. With her eyes focused on the crystal vase sitting quietly on her dark coffee table, she was unaware of throwing the handset and smashing her prized possession into smithereens.

With tears streaming from wide open eyes, Sandra mourned for herself, for her career, for the feeling that she was dissolving into a familiar nightmare. One in which she was back in Lockport High School being told she hadn't been accepted by the editors to work on the school paper. The school paper was managed by the "in" crowd. And they made it clear they hadn't wanted her as a member of their click. For the balance of her senior year she shrouded herself in a world of solitude, ignoring the over-indulged crowd. In hindsight it hadn't been all that hard. They didn't travel in the same circles. Sandra lived in the poorer section of town, the only area her mother could afford on her cleaning lady's salary. These girls lived in the wealthier neighborhoods. By not seeking to be their friend, she avoided comparisons of wardrobe, neighborhood, and lack of friends. It had been the first of many rules she set out to live by. Don't seek the approval of others, she could only rely on herself. For the remainder of high school, Sandra watched and noted everything the popular girls wore and did. She was in training to be the best. Someday, she'd return and show them up. She'd be successful, beautiful, and financially well off.

Rousing herself, Sandra saw the devastation. It was like a series of slashes on a perfect photograph. She grabbed a dust pan and brush from the kitchen and began sweeping glass into the kitchen garbage pail. Having swept all she could, she took out the vacuum cleaner and went over the carpet three times before vacuuming the pristine sofa, chairs, adjacent dining room, and kitchen floors. Satisfied that her perfect world had been restored she returned the vacuum to the hall closet. Only then did she remove her coat and hang it on its customary hanger. All of the hangers in the hall closet were evenly spaced, no more, no less, than ¾ of an inch apart, one hanger for each garment, no extras to take up space.

With the suitcase forgotten, Sandra headed for her bedroom where she disrobed, laying her clothes on an upholstered bench at the foot of her king size bed. Turning and walking into her bathroom, she took a sleeping pill while staring at her naked torso in the medicine cabinet mirror. She looked the same. No older. Still slim. Even her makeup had remained in place after her twenty hour flight. Turning off the bathroom light she got into bed, pulled the satin spread back and crawled between the crisply ironed cotton sheets. Closing her eyes and taking a few deep breaths, she slowed her racing heart and little by little fell into a drugged sleep.

24

Sparkey was still at his office computer, trying to trace the information Katherine had found in the company's files. A trip to Andorra was the most interesting development as it was one of the least known countries with friendly banking institutions. A small country between France and Spain, he didn't think it had signed a formal extradition treaty with the US. It would be ideally suited for Victor to hide his ill-gotten gains. Another interesting tidbit was Victor's middle name, Charles, also the name of his father. Was his choice of pseudonym a tribute to his father? Sparky now had the "V" for Victor and "C" for Mr. Charles, the registered owner of VC Services.

"Where is his personal information?" Sparkey remarked to himself. Thomas had once asked him to research the background of a job candidate. It turned out he was an illegal. So he had firsthand experience in Marathon's rigorous screening of job candidates. Why then was Victor Charles Rosso's file so sketchy?

The ringing phone had him looking at his watch. It was almost nine on a Friday evening. Who in Hell would know he was still at the office?

"Sparks."

"It's Jake. I've found the girl. Her name is Marilyn Wong. She's a call girl who hangs out at the bar of Westside Inn. That's where I filmed Mr. Abbott. She should be there now. Do you want to meet me there?"

"Absolutely, let's say in twenty minutes. How did you find her?"

"When I left filming that little play, I checked the hotel registry. Just in case this sick video came back to haunt me. Remember I gave you the name of an Asian woman on the hotel registry? Well, I began my search for her at the hotel bar."

"Good thinking. I'm on my way. Oh, Jake, can you copy the edited video to your cell?"

"Better, I'll load both versions on my iPad. Will you want me to film our little ambush?"

Great idea. Can you use your smallest camera? I don't want her spooked or know what we're up to."

"Yup. In twenty then."

*　　　*　　　*

As Sparkey walked up to the hotel entrance, Jake stepped out from the shadows. "How do you want to handle this?"

"I'm going to approach her as a potential client. Offer to buy her a drink and suggest we sit at a table. You walk over and join us. We don't have time for niceties, so I'm going to threaten her into giving us the creep's name."

Sparkey entered the low lit cocktail lounge noting it was populated with a scattering of men dressed in business clothes and an occasional man and woman sharing a drink at the bar. There she sat, alone at one end of the bar. Walking over and sitting on the adjacent stool, he looked like any of the other businessmen in the room.

"Bartender, I'll have a bottle of lager." He gave the girl a warm smile. "May I buy you a drink? I'm in town for the evening and would like some company."

"I'll have a Martini."

Sparkey expected her to proposition him. Instead, she sat silently fingering a silver bracelet with some Chinese characters inscribed on the band. She was little more than a living skeleton, the bracelet far too big for her bone-thin wrist. When the drinks arrived and he had paid the bartender, Sparkey turned towards the girl. If she was a pro, why wasn't she showing interest in either him or her newly arrived drink? If she needed his business, Sparkey thought she would at the least thank him for the drink.

In a low voice guaranteed not to be overheard, he said, "Why don't you join me at that table over in the corner? We can get to know one another." Stepping to one side, Sparkey watched the lithe movements of the child-like girl as she walked to the table he'd chosen for privacy. Since she hadn't picked up her drink, he carried it to the table, maneuvering her to an inside chair. Placing the drink in front of this indifferent young girl, Sparkey sat in a chair next to her just as Jake approached and sat alongside, boxing the girl in between them.

"Hey what is this?" she asked, her previously vacant expression now one of discomfort.

"A conversation between business associates. We are going to show you a film and you are going to give us the name of the director." Watching as the girl squirmed, Sparkey noticed her looking over to the side of the bar where two goons stood looking in her direction. It was the same two in Jake's video.

"Don't get any ideas about calling your friends to join us." And with that, he signaled Jake to show the original video. Jake started the video and sat hunched over, hiding it from view of the thugs across the room.

While the bar had a low hum of conversation, the table was as quiet as a morgue. Marilyn Wong sat focused on the unfolding film. Sparkey could see her escalating alarm, with her young body rigid and increased fingering of her bracelet. When the video stopped, she sat silently hugging her arms across her chest withdrawing into some private world.

"Marilyn, were you aware that you had been starring in this little movie?"

"How do you know my name?" If her pale complexion could have blanched paler than white, it didn't show. But the biting of her lower lip was all the indication Sparkey needed. She may not have known she was being filmed, but she knew something. "So, how did you get this gentleman into that room?"

Jake had just clicked on the edited video and turned the iPad toward the frightened girl. As Sparkey watched the girl for some reaction, he began to suspect she was a pawn in someone's sick game. Her reactions had escalated from fear to outright terror, not the responses of a pro involved in setting a trap.

Marilyn's hand shook as tried to swallow her Martini, most of which had slopped over the edge of her glass. Sparkey was sure it was little more than water. He doubted she would have gulped her drink in the same way if it were mainly vodka.

"A regular customer asked me to do him a favor. All he wanted was for me to give a man a call and tell him that I had some information from his Hong Kong representative. This customer said he was playing a joke on a friend."

"And you invited him to this cozy place? Then what?"

"I was to slip a ruffie into his drink and then help him to my room upstairs. Honestly, that's all I was told to do."

"And those two fine men near the bar just showed up? We watched you call them."

Nodding, Marilyn looked over to the bartender and signaled for a drink. Sparkey saw the hand signal and the bartender's nod before pouring her drink and knew it was something she had done before. She certainly was a pretty young thing. Slim, clear brown eyes, and nicely dressed for someone in her profession. Sparkey wasn't sure how long she had been in the game, but he saw that she still had some pride. It showed in her choice of a plain dress, simple makeup, and her fear of the two thugs who never took their eyes off her. If she'd hardened, she wouldn't have cared how she looked, and would have handled herself more shrewdly when they had shown her the first film. She'd probably have told them to fuck off, or she'd call the thugs and have them thrown out.

"Marilyn, how did you get yourself into this business? You seem smart and certainly beautiful." Watching to see if his comments would inspire an honest exchange, he saw her eyes soften. Maybe by not threatening her but helping her out of this trap, he would get her trust.

The bartender arrived with her drink, and this time it had olives and one cube. Paying him, Sparkey watched as Marilyn sipped at the vodka and set it carefully on the table. She looked at Jake, closed her eyes for a moment then nodded. "It's a bitch of a life. I have no choice. I'm illegal."

Sparkey understood her plight. She was probably tricked into the trade, promised a green card, and a new life in America. "Marilyn, do you have a place to go if you were deported?"

"I'd go home to Hong Kong and marry my childhood boyfriend. I'd leave in a shot...if I could. I've no money, and I'm closely watched by those two over there."

"I'll help you go home if you help us. But we don't have much time. I can promise you that I'll take you away from those two. Will you help me identify the person behind this setup?"

"Helping you could get me killed," she said. "You see those two, they keep me under control by threatening my life. Being deported isn't in their plans."

"And you are safe as long as you obey their rules." Sparkey said.

Picking up her drink, Marilyn gave another sip. "I tried to get away once. I can still feel the beating. Oh they didn't hurt my face, but my entire body was so badly bruised it looked tattooed. I couldn't move for a week."

"I promise to get you back to Hong Kong if you help us." Sparkey saw a shift in the girl's expression.

"My customer is a business man. He stops by once a week, usually on Saturday around 11 pm. I call him Honey. He never gave me a name."

"And you expect him tomorrow evening?"

"Yes. He's not into anything kinky. All he wants is a massage and blow job followed by a short cuddle. If only my life were always that easy."

"OK. This is what we are going to do. You go on as usual. I will set up your flight home for tomorrow evening. Keep your luggage to a minimum. I have a friend who flies private charters to Hong Kong and will add you to his travel group. Once you are safely in Hong Kong, he will make sure you are taken to a friendly airport security guard. My friend has helped other girls in your situation. You can trust him."

Sparkey saw that Marilyn Wong had made a decision to trust him. *Does she have any choice?* He thought.

"Now, your customer. Before he arrives tomorrow, we will be hiding in the room next to yours. Can you give us your room number?"

"It's the same room."

"I've got it, Sparkey."

"Fine. Marilyn, we'll arrive at 10:30 and wait for you to finish with this customer. Try to finish early. Then when he leaves, I'll take you to my friend. Can you leave without your shadows spotting you?"

"They won't look for me for an hour. If I can get my customer to leave before then, all I'll have to do is go down the back stairs."

"Good, I will meet you in the hall and have a taxi waiting to take both of us to the airfield. Don't worry, I'll give you all the information tomorrow. "

"But customs? I have no papers."

"It is a private airfield and a small group of passengers. Don't worry, I will introduce you to my friend and he will make sure you won't be checked. Once you land he will usher you past Hong Kong customs." Seeing that she was skeptical, he said, "Really. Tomorrow, you will be safely on your way home."

Sparkey hoped that would be true. Hong Kong customs had to be a better choice than being a sex slave. As he started to rise, she grabbed his hand. "Hey. You can't leave now. I have to take you up to my room. You have to pay me $200 for the hour. See those two watching me? If I don't give them your money in fifteen minutes, they'll beat me bloody."

Sparkey had at one time or another played the role of a john. While not his favorite disguise, he should have remembered that for Marilyn to spend time with any man, she had to be paid so she could turn over her earnings to her employer. Nodding to Jake, he rose to leave, his arm around the girl's waist and together like new found friends, headed for her room upstairs.

*   *   *

Jake rushed back home to transfer the recording he made of their meeting with Marilyn on to a disk. Then he had to gather his equipment for the following night's work. He'd book the room he'd used last time. Marilyn said she was assigned the same room for all of her clients. Jake wondered if she lived there as well.

If he could help Sparkey find a connection between Marilyn and her regular client, it would give them someone to follow. He had to know who had planned this whole sick scene. Hell with the law. He was itching to punch the creep's lights out. But Sparkey seemed on the level so he'd remind the man that by joining him as he filmed the girl and her john, he was engaging in a criminal act. Somehow, Jake didn't think it would matter. Sparkey was like a dog with a bone. Hadn't he said this was personal?

25

Feeling that something wasn't quite right, the stout man bent over his computer, rechecking his bank accounts. The two Andorra accounts and smaller one in the Cayman Islands were balanced. His New York bank had just posted his quarterly interest, but that was expected. "I can't wait to get out of this country. I should be getting 4% not ¼%." He always talked to himself when stressed.

Picking up the evening paper, he saw a news item reporting that the United States government had been increasing the number of agreements with countries like those with Switzerland, Lichtenstein, and Belize, to report all bank accounts held by US citizens. In 2014 the IRS would begin levying severe financial penalties on US citizens not declaring an off shore account of more than $30,000. The regulators were now looking into Bitcoins, the controversial non-bank currency trading over the internet. So far Bitcoin currency had its glitches, but the lure of keeping owners anonymous, was fueling international interest. *Wasn't the government ever satisfied? Next are they are going to implant a microchip into all new born baby's and track them from birth to death?*

I better move up my departure. First, close down VC Services by reducing the monthly fee before terminating the company's contract. In that way I can avoid unwanted attention. Next book a quick trip to Andorra. I have to purchase a home, file for citizenship papers and get an identity card. Once I have a residence I can begin shipping my personal property a little at a time. I don't want my nosy building superintendent asking questions.

Before he did anything else he had to transfer the $800,000 into untraceable cash. His options were diminishing with the government's attention to off-shore banking by US citizens.

During his previous arrangements with Miguel, the son of an electronics store owner, he learned that the kid had several side businesses for which he accepted only cash. Originally he hired Miguel to secure all of his international online activities. It was the young genius who had introduced him to the untraceable Hong Kong online service. Now, he needed to find a way to transfer the $800,000 from the Cayman bank while keeping his identity a secret.

"Hello Miguel, I need to visit your back office."

"How is 10 pm?"

"Fine. See you then."

*   *   *

The alley was dark and if he hadn't been here before, he was sure he'd need either a bodyguard or a gun to feel safe. As he approached a dark and dented metal back door, it opened revealing the intense young man greeting him with a silent nod. As he looked around Miguel's unofficial office, he saw that it was poles apart from his dad's long established retail operation of well-lit displays featuring the latest in computer and other electronic equipment.

The downtown area around New York's City Hall was known for its discounted electronics retailers. Miguel's store had been built by his father in the 50s, having escaped Castro's Cuba with ambitions to provide a new and better life for his family.

Miguel had told him he grew up with the business. "Dad was a hard task master, continually watching and pushing me to do more. The message was if I studied and worked hard, I'd succeed in America."

The man had worked with Miguel on enough occasions to learn that the kid had been in grade school when he discovered computers, and everything changed when his father began to consult him about the fast growing area of technology.

Known to Miguel as Mr. Charles, he had only recently learned that the smart-ass kid ran a parallel operation from the building's storeroom. Now as he looked around the dusty room in which all equipment shone bright as new, he surmised this guarded kid had been stashing away more money than he'd ever dreamed of earning with the family's legitimate business.

"Miguel, can you provide me with a stored value card?"

"How do you know about stored value cards? Or, that I can help you?" the kids surly response triggered caution.

Carefully studying the intense face challenging him, he replied, "I overheard you helping a customer with a similar, much larger request." Mr. Charles could see the younger man's wheels spinning trying to decide if he was trustworthy.

"I remember you saying that you provided stored value cards to thieves who wanted to hide the cash they received for stolen goods. The amounts were anywhere from $25 to $1,000. Since you know me, I hoped you would help me convert $800,000 from cash to an untraceable card."

"How do you plan to give me the funds? I can't hide that amount of cash."

He'll do it! He had all he could do to contain his excitement. "I can deliver it via a wire transfer from a numbered Cayman bank account to any intermediary of your choice. If you have access to a similar account, there won't be any trail."

"I can work with that." Miguel replied.

"Satisfy my curiosity and tell me how." Mr. Charles had been building his fortune for years and thought he knew all the tricks for hiding his wealth. The store value card was something he'd never heard of and wanted to learn all he could before using one.

"Let's just say I've set up several accounts in the Cayman Islands to wash money. No larger than mail drops, each company maintains an active and complex system to transfer wealth. This service is for my special customers who want to move large amounts of cash out of the country."

He nodded. If by customers he meant drug dealers, his $800,000 was a mere pittance.

Following Miguel to a small office, he watched the kid boot up his computer. "I'm going to have to charge you 2% for this little service." Miguel said indicating he'd not accept no for an answer.

Nodding his approval, Mr. Charles observed Miguel entering his coded banking information into his system, then turned the monitor over to him. Upon entering his account information, both men watched as the funds left one account and appeared in the other.

Miguel pulled up another program and in minutes produced a plastic card similar to a credit card in appearance. "Unlike a department store card containing information about its owner, this card's microchip contains only the cards fiscal balance. It's as good as cash and can be used for purchases anywhere in the world. Since the transaction leaves both banks for an unknown destination, the transfer of funds takes place outside of the banking system. With no records of a destination the card becomes virtually untraceable." Miguel explained.

Reaching for the bit of plastic, Mr. Charles studied the plain blue face. There were no identifying marks, only some corporate looking graphic. Holding it gingerly at first, he began to caress it knowing he held magic. With the everyday look of a credit card, but totally untraceable, he had found way to hide his recent ill-gotten gains.

"Amazing. It was so easy. Can I check this out?" he asked the kid.

"Sure, swipe it on this machine, but don't enter an amount. Simply remove the card and cancel the transaction."

Again studying the little plastic wafer before he did as instructed, his grin widened at seeing that his $800,000, less the $16,000 fee, appear on the screen of the little machine. "Thank you, Miguel. This will come in handy."

With his business completed he placed the card in his wallet along with his driver's license and credit cards, and left the building reminding himself to transfer the remaining $200,000 in the account to Andorra. Grabbing a taxi he rode home to contemplate his riches.

*   *   *

It was after midnight when his flights to and from Andorra had been booked and he had electronically transferred the remaining Cayman bank balance to Andorra. Knowing he no longer had to worry about having his financial transactions in Andorra traced by government watchdogs had him rubbing his hands together with glee.

Next step in his planning was how to use the money card to purchase his new residence in one of the best international enclaves. On a previous visit he had traveled to a gated community just outside the city, and looking at the groomed homes behind security gates, he envisioned his new life. He wanted to live in a home that said wealth, but not so elaborate that it would cause suspicion. The real estate agent had given him cost estimates of several properties and knew he could afford to buy a home befitting his new persona. One in which he would greet wealthy international friends, standing alongside his yet to find, fashionable young wife. Women and dating had never fit in his current life. In Andorra he would make time to find his trophy wife.

Looking around the library, he began a mental catalogue of his possessions. All that he valued was in this room. He'd be taking his prized Chippendale mirror, small Chinese lacquer chest, oriental inspired area rug, and his desk and custom built chair that fit his stocky body. He'd build his new home around his love of Oriental furnishings. Dark wood cabinets and tables featuring prized porcelain figurines. All upholstered furniture custom designed so his feet touched the floor, and the décor designed by a local artisan he'd met by accident when window shopping on an earlier exploratory visit to Andorra. This particular designer had entrée into the best of homes, and Charles planned to use him for an introduction to the local social scene.

Aside from his books, clothes, and papers, there was nothing of value in the rest of his apartment. He'd call a theatrical charity and arrange to have them pick up his entire kitchen, bedroom and his few upholstered living room pieces. It would close out his responsibility to the memory of his father, who before his death had depended upon this particular charity for assistance. He'd died a lonely man, left by his wife when he could no longer provide her with financial support. His looks lost to drink. His theatrical friends no longer willing or able to shore him up with bit parts or handouts.

He picked up a legal pad and began to list the packing supplies he would want delivered. He'd want to begin packing knowing it would take time to sort through and destroy any and all incriminating paperwork. That done, he made another list of everything he owned. One column, listing things to get rid of, and a second of things to be packed and shipped.

As for the larger picture, he realized he had already accomplished a lot. First to do an analysis of his financial holdings, then obtain a money card, and finally the purchase of airline tickets to Andorra. He never understood people who could live their lives one day at a time. He attributed his success in life to careful planning. Something he learned as a child, in spite of his parents.

26

Jake met Sparkey in the same room of the Westside Hotel that he had used to film Marilyn with Edward Abbott.

"How long will you need from the time I leave with the girl to clear out of here?" Sparkey asked.

"I didn't bring as much equipment this time, so I can be out in five minutes."

"You had better make it as fast as possible. Those thugs will be snooping around when Marilyn doesn't show up with their money." Thinking of the rest of their timetable, he asked, "How long will it take for you to deliver the footage to my office?"

"I can slip it under your office door before you get back from the airport. I'll make a copy first, just to be sure we don't lose the information, and I'll leave you the original footage. It's all on a disk, not videotape, so it will play on any computer."

"Good. That way no one can accuse us of doctoring the film."

Sparkey had arranged with Marilyn to try to shorten her client's visit to forty-five minutes, explaining, "We will be in the room next to you, and as soon as he leaves, I'll escort you down the back stairs and take you to the airport. There will be plenty of time for me to brief you on the way. We are going to a small suburban airport serving Westchester. The flight is a charter, and the group is a small private tour heading to Hong Kong. You can trust my friend to see that you are returned home safely."

Marilyn had told him that her guards would become suspicious if she didn't appear back in the bar with her money within one hour, the time she normally used to service this particular client. Because he was a regular, they wouldn't check on her before then.

Sparkey, nodded, understanding how closely she was watched. "That's why you need to get him to leave at least ten minutes early. More, if possible. Can you do that?"

"He won't be difficult. I'll be on time." Marilyn said.

Jake took Sparkey aside. "Hey man, before we start I have to warn you that what we're doing is illegal."

Sparkey squeezed the young man's shoulder. "I know. I'll take care of both of us. Promise."

*　　　*　　　*

"Well, now we wait." Jake said, as he adjusted the camera so it would capture the entire room.

Sparkey prayed they would be able to identify the blackmailer. That would give Thomas leverage in shutting the guy up and recovering the $800,000 before the beginning of business on Monday. So far they had prevented anyone outside the small concerned group from learning of the blackmail and embezzlement of funds from the Sweeney Family Foundation. If tonight was successful, and Marilyn's client was someone inside Marathon, Sparkey could strike before the rat could do additional harm.

"Here we go Sparkey." Jake said, as the camera began to film the room next door. "You can get a camera's-eye view in this separate view finder."

Sparkey moved closer and looking through the view finder tried to get a good look at the man Marilyn had escorted into the room. His vision was blocked by the man's back as he stood facing the girl while his hands began to roam over her slim body. *Hell this could take all night*, Sparkey thought. *When she said all he wanted was a blow job and cuddle, I was expecting her to get him right on the bed.*

Sparkey's frustration increased as Marilyn slowly opened the man's jacket and slipping it off laid it on the nearby chair. *Was the man impotent? He's just letting her undress him.* Still taking her time, Marilyn slowly striped the man from his shirt, pants, underwear, and shoes leaving him standing naked in short black socks.

As Sparkey continued to watch the unfolding drama, the short plump body slowly backed up and sat on the edge of the bed. "Turn around you beast." Sparkey whispered to himself. "That's right, a little more." Just when Sparkey's frustration had reached its limits, Marilyn pushed the naked man back on the bed, and with little effort had him stretch out full length on his back. As Marilyn began to mount him, Sparkey, thought *Holy Shit!* Not believing what he saw, his gaze continued to follow the girl's ministrations that shortly brought the man to climax.

"You recognize this creep?" Jake asked.

"Yup." Picking up his cell he dialed Thomas. "Our blackmailer is Rosso. I'll have film for you later tonight. See you at your house. You'd better have the scotch poured. You won't be able to after seeing the footage."

27

Knowing that Edward had been having trouble sleeping, Megan tried to distract him from worrying himself sick. Between them they hadn't come up with even one possibility of who had set out to destroy him.

"Sweetheart, if you can't sleep, why not read about a real criminal? How about that book by Diana B. Henriques, *Wizard of Lies: Bernie Madoff and the Death of Trust?*"

Edward turned toward his wife, shaking his head. "That certainly would be a distraction. To see how someone who actually committed a breach of fiduciary trust thinks. Maybe it will help at my trial? After all I only stole $800,000 from a foundation devoted to good works, it's not stealing from individual investors."

"Don't you even think about this going to trial."

"Darling, what I did was not only illegal but immoral. I deserve to be tried and sentenced by a jury."

"No you don't. Thomas is working hard on finding the pieces to put this horror behind all of us. I trust him with my life and yours."

Hugging her husband close, Megan prayed her confidence in her uncle and his love of puzzling out problems would find the bastard who wrought so much damage. It had shaken Edward's confidence. Her husband was the kind of man who remained the calm focal point regardless of the crisis. When Marathon had begun to move the company's headquarters to New York, Edward had faced a threatened walkout by the manufacturing arm of the company. Standing firm, he negotiated with the head of the employees committee and reached a solution accepted by both sides. Always calm, never threatening, Edward compromised where possible, and convinced employees when necessary of the reasons behind the company's stand on specific issues. To his credit, Marathon remained a non-union company.

Wishing this situation were over, Megan knew without proving he'd been setup and returning the stolen funds, the love of her life would never be the same. If that were to happen, she feared for them both.

*   *   *

The ringing phone jolted Megan out of a deep sleep. "Yes?" she answered and saw that her bedside clock read 1 am.

"Hello darling, I'm truly sorry to wake you but I think we have our rat trapped. Can you calm Edward down and be at the house at two this afternoon?" Thomas asked.

"Today, Sunday?"

"That's right. Now go back to sleep and I'll see you later."

Looking over at her husband who looked prepared to meet the grim reaper, Megan pulled him down on the bed and gave him a full body hug. "That was Uncle Thomas. To quote him accurately, 'I think we have our rat trapped.' He wants us at the house at two today."

Edward hugged her hard enough to break a rib, and Megan felt the gush of his tears of relief on her neck. "Sweetheart," she whispered as she held her husband close. "We're going to be fine. Hush now…we're safe and soon we'll be able to slam the door on this entire incident."

28

Sparkey had arrived back from the small airport after having turned Marilyn Wong over to his friend for safe delivery back to her home country. Just as he started to check his computer Jake walked in and handed him a disk. Sparkey opened a beer and placed it in the young man's hand. "Relax. For now you are home free."

"I'm truly out of this snake pit?" Jake said, and took a swig from the frosty bottle. Seeing Sparkey's nod in confirmation, he sagged into the soft chair, all six foot plus of his long legs stretched out before him. "You don't need me?"

"Well, how good are you on computers? Can you hack into Victor Rosso's home computer?"

"Sure. What do you have in mind?"

"Later today there's going to be a show down," he said while waving the disk Jake had just handed him for emphasis. "At the conclusion of a little show-and-tell performance, we are going to escort this creep home and you are going to see that he returns all the money he's blackmailed and embezzled from Marathon Nutritionals. But first we have to know where he has it hidden. I don't believe he's only focused on extorting money from Edward Abbott. If I did, the amount would be more like $3 million, not $800,000. We now know that our rat has also been stealing from the company for years. We just don't know why he wants to ruin Edward or where the money is."

"Marathon Nutritionals? That's your friend's company?"

"Yup. And you are going to love the bit of theater my friend has cooked up. Are you in?" Seeing a spark of life in the tired young man, Sparkey paused. In working with the kid, Sparkey found him to be more than his considerable talents. And he just plain liked him. Knowing Jake hated the entire sordid business, Sparkey wanted to be sure this part of the kid's life got left in the past.

"I'm in." he said, taking another sip of beer. "Sparkey, what happened to the girl?"

"She got to you too?"

"Yeah. She seemed so young. Did she tell you how long she'd been turning tricks for those goons?"

"We had a brief chat on the way to the airport. It seems she'd only been here a couple of months. Hopefully she can eventually put all of this out of her mind and resume a normal life." Sparkey replied.

"What kind of life will she have in Hong Kong?"

"Apparently, her parents run a restaurant. She said she didn't care if she cleaned fish for the rest of her life, she'd just be grateful to be home."

"How is your friend going to sneak her past immigrations?" Jake asked.

"When I briefed Stan on her situation and need to escape, he told me that he has helped other unfortunate illegals back to their home countries. When he heard how Marilyn had been tricked into prostitution, he assured me that he'd personally see to it that she arrived back home without fuss. Once she's there it's up to her."

"I guess she's smart enough to cut any ties to the people who brought her to this country. I'd hate to see her trapped again. She reminds me of a girl I went to grade school with. Her father was pimping her out. I just want her to get a chance at a real life!" Jake explained.

"Let's hope she can. My friend said the travel business he runs has certain freedoms from border checks and customs. Without his saying so, I am guessing he has friends at the airport who will help."

*   *   *

Jake had been at Sparkey's office computer for the past two hours when he finally hacked into Victor Rosso's home computer. Finding a file containing his personal financial records, Jake printed out a listing of locations and amounts in each of Rosso's bank accounts. While he couldn't access the accounts, he was able to identify the location and amounts in four separate banks located in New York City, Cayman Islands and two in Andorra.

Reading the detailed printout of Rosso's financial life, Sparkey exclaimed, "Thank you God, He's a compulsive record keeper."

"Andorra? Where in hell is it? This is a new one on me." Jake said.

"I've only read about it. But it is another country with liaise faire attitudes on keeping bank records of foreign nationals."

"I'll have to have passwords and login codes in order to gain access to each of these accounts. Unless you plan to trust this rat, to voluntarily fork over his ill-gotten gains."

"Not to worry my friend. Meet me here at 1:30. By the end of this afternoon's gathering, you and I will escort this bastard home. Then, you will get your chance to access each of those accounts and recover the missing funds."

*　　　*　　　*

It took everything Thomas Sweeney had in him to keep his voice light. "Hello, Victor. I realize it's after midnight, but I wanted to call and alert you to a meeting I'm having at my home at 2:30 today. I have decided to make some changes in preparing for the company's future listing on the stock exchange. As COO, I will value your contributions."

"Today at 2:30 it is. Do you want me to bring the quarterly plans and budgets?" Victor said.

"That won't be necessary. I have your previous information on my computer. See you later. Victor, I'm sure you will find this meeting of particular interest."

29

Thomas Sweeney had a lifetime of dealing with self-important people. He didn't suffer fools and made sure none would be part of his company. Aside from Megan and Edward, Marathon Nutritionals was his family.

Knowing the confrontation with Rosso had to be a swift strike, Sweeney girded himself for the role he liked least, that of an intimidating bastard. They had worked together for almost a decade. How could he have so misjudged the man?

Thomas had given in to his explosive anger once before, as a young medic in the army. It was when a lieutenant, a few years his junior, demanded that one of his patients be immediately returned to duty. Sweeney, the medic in charge, was trying to make sure his young patient didn't lose the use of his arm. He remembered being focused on wrapping the boy's wounds, when he heard the loud-mouthed officer push his nurse aside in an attempt to reach the soldier. The nurse had been at Sweeney's side for ten hours that day, working to care for torn bodies and broken bones before their patients bled-out or, died of complications. Watching aghast as the young woman picked herself up from the operating room floor, Sweeney had lost control.

"Lieutenant, get the fuck out of my operating room." Each word spoken in anger was a piece of shrapnel aimed at the obnoxious young man. Normally, he went about mending and patching men and women quietly, totally focused on the medical challenges of working against the clock to prepare the wounded for transport to hospitals for follow up care. The lieutenant abruptly turned heel, leaving the soldier behind. The speedy retreat couldn't hide the lieutenant's reddened face or glittering stare. The vision of the officer's distress and embarrassment had been forever imprinted in Sweeney's memory as a reminder to keep a lid on his temper.

During the years since that incident, Sweeney had maintained tight control over his anger. Now when he thought of that incident, he recalled how grateful he had been for the support of his operating team, who with quiet words of comfort, enabled him to quickly resume the work at hand. They had their own run-ins with self-important officers. Like Sweeney, their first duty was to the men and women in their care.

*　　　*　　　*

The library in Thomas Sweeney's townhouse was funereal. Edward and Megan sat hand-in-hand on a loveseat off to the side of his desk. Both were conservatively dressed and appeared outwardly calm. Sparkey, and his young associate Jake, were standing in front of the drape-darkened windows. Knowing Sparkey for as long as he had, Thomas knew he was on full alert. When he had asked Shen to join them, he had declined, saying, "My presence would only divert attention away from Victor's crimes. He'd think I was the reason for his being fired." There had been no preliminary discussion of the afternoon's meeting. All present knew of Victor Rosso's multiple treacheries.

Victor Rosso arrived at 2:15 and Thomas asked his butler to have him wait in the foyer. A master at staging negotiations, Thomas wanted to have the psychological advantage. The first step was to make the man physically uncomfortable. There were no chairs in the foyer. Victor would have to stand and wait. Promptly at 2:30 the butler knocked on the library door and announced the arrival of Victor Rosso. The silent group watched as Victor's swagger slowed when he saw that he wasn't the first to arrive.

"Thank you for coming Victor. Please take a seat." Signifying that Victor should sit in the straight backed chair across from his desk, Sweeney noticed that Victor, now on alert with partially closed eyes looked over each person in the room. Sweeney saw him straighten up a bit when one by one, Megan and Edward avoided his gaze. Fingering large gold cuff links on the stiff French cuffs of his shirt, he nodded first to Thomas and only then sat in the chair indicated.

After a pregnant pause, Sweeney stood up behind his desk, and in a cordial tone addressed the object of the gathering. "Victor, I have something I'd like you to see." With that he turned the desktop monitor around and started playing a video. The picture that lit up the screen showed Victor on his back with Marilyn administering her sexual services. Knowing that the entire 12-minute video wouldn't be as effective as 30 seconds of the right images, Sparkey had cued the disk to picture Marilyn bringing Rosso to orgasm.

"Are you mad?" rumbled Victor, jumping up to stop the video. Are you spying on my personal life? Well, it's not for public viewing!" He glanced over at Megan, ignoring the men in the room.

"Sit!" ordered Sweeney. "Shut the hell up." Removing the disk he inserted another, this one showing the thugs arranging the unconscious Edward and Marilyn on the hotel room bed.

Sweeney watched Victor like someone watching a snake. *What is going on in this traitor's mind?* he wondered. *Did he actually think he could blackmail Edward and steal from my company without my finding out?*

In his firmest, executive manner, Sweeney began delivering his ultimatums to the man calmly sitting before him. "Victor, you are going to resign. You are going to deposit $800,000 blackmailed funds to an account of my choosing. Additionally, you are going to donate $2,880,000 to the Sweeney Family Foundation. The exact amount you have been stealing from the company for the past eight years. Furthermore you are going to close down VC Services and add any remaining money residing in that bank account to your donation."

A sputtering Victor stood, shocking the room with his wily response. "What in hell are you talking about? That's almost three million dollars. Check my bank account. I don't have near that amount."

"Sit!" barked Sweeney, enraged by the man's attempt to discount the realities of his felonious actions.

"I demand to know who planned this ambush!" Turning towards Edward, Victor Rosso's face a study in rage, swore, "You think you're so smart. You don't even know what you don't know. All you do is add up the numbers. I'm glad you resigned. No one in their right mind would hire someone like you."

The room was deathly silent, as Victor returned to the chair he'd been forced to take on arrival.

It was clear to Thomas that Victor still felt in control. *Well that's his problem,* he thought. With steel in every word, he continued delivering his demands. "Victor, I have terminated your employment contract and order you to leave the company, effective immediately. You are never to mention this entire incident, our meeting, or your crimes to anyone. Should one word be leaked, I will turn over our documentation to the FBI. I doubt you would enjoy jail since I plan to see you incarcerated in a high security prison."

"You won't dare fire me. Not if you plan to take Marathon public!" Victor's voice dripped with venom. "Your precious company's reputation would be tarnished and Marathon would no longer be the darling of hopeful investors. What I will do is resign. Period."

As if a cat was playing with a mouse, Sweeney replied, "You misunderstand me Victor. I don't care about listing Marathon on the exchange if it means you go unpunished."

"I haven't agreed to anything. Not to your demands, and not to this meeting. I'm leaving." As Victor stood, Sparkey moved up behind him, and jerking his arm up behind his back jammed him back down on his chair.

"Victor, let me introduce you to John Sparks. Mr. Sparks is a man of many talents. I wouldn't recommend disobeying him."

As Sparkey stood over Victor with one hand gripping the man's shoulder, Sweeney continued in his take no prisoners tone, "I have a document ready for your signature. It details your crimes of embezzlement, entrapment, blackmail, and violation of your contract as an officer of Marathon Nutritionals on grounds of theft. It lists the amounts you have stolen over a period of eight years via your VC Services shell company; your association with one Marilyn Wong to ensnare Edward Abbott into a compromising situation; your blackmailing Edward; your financial history including the names, numbers and locations of your four bank accounts; and shortly we will also have a complete email record of all wire transfers of funds into and out of these banks."

Sweeney studied Victor's reactions more closely and noticed that while his skin had returned to its normal doughy color, his eyes were anything but calm. They blazed. *So*, Sweeney thought, *this is only round one.*

"I'm sure you wouldn't have me sign anything without advice of counsel. Give me a copy of this...document. I'll have my attorney look it over and get back to you." Getting up from the chair, Victor leaned over to pick up the agreement when Sweeney threw a punch and knocked him to the floor. Megan gasped. There he sat sprawled on the floor. A man who schemed to steal, blackmail and undermine all that Thomas Sweeney valued.

Standing over Victor, Sweeney wondered how he had been so blinded to the man's resentment. It must have been festering for years. Grabbing the smaller man by the shoulders to steady him on his feet, Thomas felt him cringe. "I'm not going to throw another punch. You're not worth it."

Moving back to his desk, Sweeney delivered his final salvo. "You are not leaving this room without signing these papers." He waved a thick document in Victor's face. "Should you need legal advice, I'm sure that either Edward or I can address your concerns." Pointing to his desk, Sweeney said, "There's the pen. I will give you five minutes to sign both this agreement and your confession, or I'll call the police."

Straightening up and squaring his shoulders, Victor Charles Rosso walked to the desk, picked up the pen and without reading his death warrant, signed all copies where indicated and tossed the pen aside.

Megan walked up to her former boss and in a very low voice, said, "Victor why?"

Looking at the woman who was the reason behind his hatred, he whispered, "Because you chose him over me."

30

I t was Sunday and Katherine was grateful the hellacious week was over. How Sandra Charney would react in the morning was yet to be determined.

She had carefully documented each bit of news coverage of the announcement. Her fears that the reasons behind Edwards' retirement had been leaked and would appear as page-one news, or primetime television coverage, had haunted her from the first interview. Now she could congratulate herself that the earth was aligned with the stars and the announcement had gone without a hitch.

All three reporters had stated the facts accurately. When facing tight deadlines, reporters' columns were reviewed and occasionally altered by editors who, not being familiar with the details, sometimes made mistakes. Fortunately, this time, everything presented to readers of *Time* and *The Wall Street Journal* were accurate. Her fear that the televised interview on CNN would be tainted when edited down into sound bites a few seconds each, also proved unfounded. Yes, she had done well.

Closing her mind to the events of the past week, Katherine had invited Sally over to help take her mind off work. Now sitting with her friend, Katherine's thoughts turned to Sally's social life. As they sat sipping and nibbling, a favorite alternative to eating a greasy, high calorie take out meal, they commiserated over her latest online dating disaster.

"He didn't even have the decency to offer to pay for my drink. I had one glass of bar wine, not a vintage selection, for Christ's sake!" Sally complained.

Katherine hoped that it was time Sally finally admitted that her online efforts weren't producing any appealing men. She also realized it was time for her to pay attention to her own lack of male companionship.

"Sally, you know that party I have been talking about?" She watched her friend nod as she continued grazing on a selection of vegetables set out on the coffee table. "Well, whether or not I have a job after tomorrow, I am still going to plan that party. It's just too bad I don't have even one man to contribute to the event."

"You could always invite Mike. He'd do anything for you. In fact, why don't you ever talk to him like a woman instead of a customer?"

"Mike doesn't think of me that way. After all the years we've been frequenting Malachy's, he's never even hinted that he was interested."

"You really are blind. Have you ever wondered why he chats me up and not you? He's so in love with you he has a hard time getting his words out. For a writer who breathes in words, I find that highly suspect."

"Come on, Sally, Mike and I talk all the time."

"Not as potential lovers. Do me a favor just think about it, before you plan your guest list."

"OK. I hear you. Yes, I will consider inviting Mike... even if I have to go to Malachy's and issue the invitation in person."

Unfortunately, Katherine's mind switched to thoughts of the nastier aspects of Marathon's troubles...Abbott being targeted for blackmail. *Damn it. Can't I let it go for a couple of hours? Isn't Sunday a day of rest?*

As if fate had read her thoughts, the shrill ringing of the phone had her spattering red wine on her blouse. "Now what?" She was surprised to hear Thomas Sweeney's voice.

"Katherine, I wanted to reassure you that I've spoken to Sandra and she knows about the announcement. Not the details, just what was distributed and of course your interviews. I also told her that I will require more of your time this week."

"I can't thank you enough, Thomas. Is it over? Or, will you want me to continue to work with Mr. Sparks?" Aware of Sally listening to every word, Katherine nodded to her friend, signaling she'd share what she could when she hung up.

"Actually, Katherine, I was hoping I could persuade you to make a career change. I am going to be expanding the scope of the Sweeney Family Foundation's activities. It will need the expertise of someone with your knowledge of the company and skills in corporate communications.

What I am offering is to have you work directly for the Foundation's new President, as his number two...his Executive Vice President."

Sweeney paused, and Katherine knew he was waiting for her to respond, but her mouth couldn't form words fast enough before he continued. "There would of course be a significant increase in salary and benefits." He added.

Salary hadn't even entered her mind. In her wildest dreams she could never have imagined a position she would enjoy more. "Thomas, I thought you ran the Foundation."

"Up to now I have and as a small private charity. I plan to change that. Build up its resources and expand the Foundation's scope. I am especially interested in providing our nation's poorer communities with needed healthcare facilities. In order to expand the Foundation's Charter, it will need an independent management team. In fact the new president is someone you know. It's Edward Abbott."

"How exciting! I would be honored to be part of your Foundation and look forward to working for Edward. Thank you for your confidence in me, Thomas."

"You've earned it. Katherine, for the past week I've watched you not only do an outstanding job, but step up to the plate each time I've asked for your help in putting an end to our crisis. I'd love for you to stop by my office first thing in the morning and we can discuss your new responsibilities. Good night Katherine." He paused again. "Katherine?"

"Um, yes. Definitely yes, Thomas. I will see you in the morning... and, thank you again for this opportunity. It means the world to me."

"One more thing, let us keep this between ourselves for now... along with our previous secrets. That will give me a chance to tie up loose ends."

"Yes Sir. Of course."

"Good night, Katherine."

"Good night." Katherine hung up and dropped into her chair. She couldn't imagine how this had happened. He had advanced not only her career, but saved her life. Working with the Foundation would remove her from the Marathon Nutritionals employ. In reality, while Thomas Sweeney was involved with both entities, she would be working for an entirely different organization.

"Thomas? Earth to Katherine." Sally said.

"Huh?"

"Is this the Thomas Sweeney, CEO of Marathon Nutritionals? That Thomas?"

Squirming in her chair, a sheepish Katherine looked at her friend. "Now Sally, don't jump to conclusions. My secret project was for Mr. Sweeney."

"And?"

"And he said that since he was trusting me with this situation, I should call him Thomas."

"You know that party you were thinking about, why not invite him?" Sally prompted.

"What? Sally, Mr. Sweeney's call has me all sixes and sevens. He just offered me a new job. An entirely new life!" Looking stunned, Katherine saw Sally's impatience and still couldn't verbalize her news.

"You cannot drop something as important as – 'having a new life' - on me and just sit there leaving me in the dark."

"He's offered me the position of Executive Vice President of his soon to be reorganized Sweeney Family Foundation." Seeing the pleasure light her friend's face, she added, "And, I will be number two to the new President, Edward Abbott."

"And he's liberated you from working for the Bitch. What's that expression? 'God keeps score so we don't have to?'"

Giggling and still not fully believing how her life had just changed, Katherine knew that Sally had probably just figured out just who was at the center of the secretive project. "Yes, Sally, Edward Abbott's resignation was the mysterious project. Now that he has been named to the newly created position with the Sweeney Family Foundation, everything returns to normal." Katherine hoped her intuitive friend didn't spot her lie by omission.

Something Katherine didn't want to admit was that while Sally, as an attorney, was accustomed to keeping the secrets of her clients, Katherine had lost her innocence. Now she was charged with the responsibility of protecting secrets of her own. Did she feel compromised? Or was her life under Charney a protected bubble? While she fought to have more responsibility, it was Charney who by the nature of her position, was the one charged with keeping the company's secrets.

"To us. To survival. To winning."

Katherine, filled with delight, lifted her glass and drank to Sally's toast.

"My turn. Here's to fate," Katherine said, clinking Sally's glass. Then as if she had just registered the impact of her new career path, she added, "You know, Thomas Sweeney has just determined my future, and miracle of all miracles, once again it's in my control.

31

I t was after ten Sunday evening by the time Sparkey and Jake left Victor Charles Rosso's apartment. It had been a long day, and Sparkey was tired to the roots of each hair on his head. And, it wasn't over. Reaching for his cell, he punched in Thomas's home number.

"I wondered when I'd be hearing from you." Thomas said.

"All of the stolen funds are in the process of being transferred to your attorney. The short of it is that we were able to access each of the bastard's bank accounts."

"Then Jake's earlier report about Victor's off-shore activities had been accurate?" Sweeney asked.

"Yeah. The kid's a genius at manipulating computers. But Thomas, it will take a few days to recover all of the funds. Rosso was building a life outside the country. He was invested in real estate, had a healthy brokerage account and found a way to hide $800,000 he blackmailed from Edward."

"The important thing is he's been stopped. Did you have to threaten him to get his help?"

"Well at first he screamed that he'd be bankrupt. Then, after we reminded him that the value of all four accounts was approaching $6 million, he shut up. Thomas, you didn't want to see his eyes, they were those of a killer."

"That's a lot of money. Do you know where Victor planned to go? I assume he was about to leave the country with his ill-gotten fortune?"

"Some little country between France and Spain. Andorra."

"Actually I have been there as a guest of one of our overseas distributors. It was a lovely, peaceful country. According to my friend, they were as efficient as the Swiss in their banking activities."

"Thomas your performance completely deflated that puffed up little man. But to make sure he knew we were deadly serious, I did tell him that if he even moved out of his apartment before we had recovered every cent, I would personally take him to the FBI. I think they would be very interested in his activities to avoid paying taxes."

"I don't trust him. How can we be sure he hasn't got something equally devious up his sleeve? Hatred is fueling that man's brain. And I added the fuel."

"Jake hid a camera and microphone in his apartment. So he will be keeping track of Victor's every move. And since Jake has hacked his computer we can watch his online activities and correspondence as well."

"Do you know how much he will have left?"

"Probably $3 million. But, if there isn't enough in the Andorra accounts to recover all he stole, we could tap into his Marathon Nutritionals company funded pension. I understand that it's close to another million."

"No. I don't want him penniless. I just want him neutered. To disappear. Becoming an expatriate was his life's goal and part of the reason behind his evil machinations. I want him to move to another country and forget he ever knew any of us. If we totally bankrupt him he will try to take his revenge. Sparkey, didn't you say that an accounting of all of his assets totaled a bit more than $6 million?"

"Yeah. Market value of both investments and, real estate holdings as well as his Marathon earnings. And that includes that little plastic stored value card we found by accident. It held almost all of the $800,000 he blackmailed from Edward. Clever little bit of wizardry. I'll have to show it to you."

"If that's true, he'll still have around $3 million, give or take a few dollars. That should be enough to live on. I have decided to let him keep his Marathon Nutritionals pension."

"That's very generous of you Thomas. Why?" Sparkey asked.

"I don't want the traitorous Rosso suing us for past income and benefits. We'd be exposed and Edward's problems could become public knowledge. Fortunately, we haven't begun to issue participation shares to senior executives in preparation for the company's listing on the NASDAQ. So all he'll take with him is the money he earned legally, along with the company match in his profit sharing."

"I guess that's cheap at any price to keep a rat in his hole. I think you've silenced him for now. I doubt he will do anything to jeopardize his freedom."

"I'll call Victor first thing tomorrow and give him my final terms for his departure from the company. That I have released his pension, including the company match, in recognition of his past work on behalf of the company. I will verify his employment, but not give him a reference should he seek employment with another firm either in this country or abroad. And I will not prosecute him if he keeps to the terms of our separation agreement."

"Thomas, be sure to record that call just in case we need ammunition to silence him in the future. Make sure you have his verbal agreement not to divulge his plans to ruin Edward. And, if possible, get him to state that he acknowledges your generous termination package."

"Sparkey, you are asking for the moon. I've worded his termination agreement to include protection for not only Marathon, but Edward, Megan, and myself. His vendetta was personal. I wanted his signature attesting to the totality of his treachery. But I will remind him that the agreement extends to them as well. Having a recording of his consenting to my terms should help if he decides not to keep his word."

"Good thinking, friend."

"Sparkey, I need some sleep. I'm meeting with Katherine in the morning. She's accepted her new position. I'm glad she'll no longer be working with Sandra. From what Megan was able to find out, it was like working in a strait jacket."

"Speaking of that bright, lovely young woman, now that she will be working for Edward at the Foundation, why not consider changing your relationship to a more informal one?" Sparkey said.

"Sparkey, that's a maybe. Don't push me."

"One more thing, Thomas, how are you going to deal with Victor's assistant, Mary Johnson?"

"I have to think about that. She did process the VC Services invoices. I know Mary, and with Victor being such a secretive fellow, it's doubtful she was actually aware of any of his machinations."

"I had to ask. If she's innocent, I wouldn't want her to suffer for her boss's greed. Good night, Thomas."

Hanging up, Thomas wondered where he'd find someone qualified to handle the COO's responsibilities. This time he would have all candidates vetted twice over. It had to be someone he could trust and rely on to handle the position with skill and dedication. He didn't want another Victor in his life. As for Mary Johnson's future, he'd leave that up to the discretion of Victor's successor. Stretching out in bed he had a sudden brainstorm, and smiling, fell into a much needed sleep.

32

As Katherine entered the office suite, Thomas Sweeney rose from behind his desk. He strode toward her with a big smile and gave her a firm but friendly handshake. "I can't tell you how pleased I am that you have decided to jump ship and work with Edward at the Foundation. Between the two of you I am expecting an entirely refreshed and repurposed organization."

The early Monday morning was bright with promise. Taking the chair he offered, Katherine was reminded this was where one week ago her life began to change. Laughing, so very pleased by the man's enthusiasm, she had all she could do to keep from asking her millions of questions. Watching him hold up his hand to stop her onslaught had become a familiar gesture. In the short period of one week, Thomas had come to know her well enough to halt her in mid thought.

"Katherine, before we discuss your new position I want to know if you have any thoughts or questions about our recent predicament? You must realize how important your assistance has been not only to me, but to John Sparks and Dr. Lu. Edward and Megan of course can't thank me enough for my engaging you in helping to resolve this crisis."

"Thank you…Thomas, for your vote of confidence. It has been a different sort of challenge of my skills. Hopefully, I will never again be faced with something like Victor Rosso's treachery."

"On that we both agree." Thomas seemed to study her face for a minute. "Out with it. What is troubling that racing mind of yours?"

Katherine caught herself smiling at being so transparent. "Actually I'd like to fill in some blanks. It's been an unusual week during which I gleaned some information, but didn't get the pieces that led to Edward Abbott being set up for blackmail. I surmised that Victor Rosso was behind Edward's difficulties. What I don't know is why, where the money went, or if we can be sure that this mess is over and will never become public?"

She watched as this normally composed man's face showed a range of emotion from annoyance to thoughtfulness. "You should be brought up to date. I owe you that at the very least." As he unwound his long body into the chair opposite, Thomas Sweeney considered his words before speaking.

"Katherine, because I trust you, I will answer your questions with the knowledge that you will continue to keep our secrets." She nodded in agreement. "OK. First, where did the money go? Apparently Victor has been planning for an early retirement and moving to Andorra to live the life of a wealthy expatriate. He began skimming money from the company about eight years ago using a shell company that you had spotlighted during your visit with Dr. Lu."

"VC Services? The OSHA compliant cleaning company?"

"Yes. Over the years his theft amounted to the considerable sum of almost three million dollars."

"But why? He was a trusted senior executive and well paid. He had stature within the company. What else did he need?"

"I don't really think it was all about the money. Victor just felt it was something he was owed. Something I owed him. I don't even think he thought of it as detrimental to the company. After all, from his point-of-view, he was responsible for overseeing the physical running of our growing operations. I think that in his eyes, the $30,000 per month he skimmed from Marathon was insignificant. He was simply focused on building a wealthy future abroad."

"What about setting up Mr. Abbott? Was that also for money?"

"I admire your curiosity, Katherine. And to be frank you have earned the truth. As unpleasant as it is." Thomas leaning closer, confided, "I'm afraid, that in the case of blackmailing Edward, Victor's scheming was personal. He felt that Edward not only married the one woman he desired, but that I favored Edward over him. Not being aware of his jealousy, of his need to be continually praised for his contributions to the company, I may have intensified his feelings of being unappreciated. So VC Services was one way to get even with me for what he felt was my insufficient attention."

"I don't understand. He reported only to you. You treated him as you do most all employees, in a professional...if somewhat distant manner." Shit! She hadn't meant to be that blunt.

The corner of Thomas' mouth turned up. "Distant? Yes, I'm not very good at making friends with people I work with. You are reminding me that I should work on that. Of course, Edward and Megan are family. According to Victor, that meant I excluded him from my inner circle." A sudden look of anger crossed his face. "The man would never be close to me or anyone. He bred dislike by his very personality. He dictated to people, never engaged them in the decision making process. I should have suspected him of deeper issues before this. I knew Shen Lu considered him a bean counter and not someone he particularly liked. Unfortunately I didn't look for evidence that Victor was capable of corrupt behavior toward me or the company. If I had, it would have saved all of us a lot of grief."

"I can see where his self-worth would be measured by access to you. It goes with the territory. Ambitious men want to be close to power."

"You continue to surprise me, Katherine. That is a well-drawn picture of the man."

"I assume that Mr. Rosso is no longer with Marathon. What I would love to know is how he was silenced…if he has been?"

Thomas rose, and indicating that he was going to pour a cup of coffee saw her nod that she would like one as well. "Victor is a lesson in money laundering. Mr. Sparks found he had several off-shore bank accounts that were growing nicely. Those, along with the money he blackmailed from Edward, amounted to nearly $6 million."

"Katherine, Mr. Sparks is really the person who has all the details. In fact, I would like you to join John Sparks, Edward and Megan, Shen Lu and myself at a small celebratory dinner I'm hosting tomorrow evening at seven at the Union Club."

Katherine didn't know if she was more excited that Thomas had just invited her to dinner, or considered her part of his inner circle. "Certainly, I would love to celebrate with your friends. I must say I feel like I've been involved in the plotting of a mystery novel. Unfortunately, it is a case of real life…poisoned by envy and avarice. What about that scandalous video? Did Mr. Sparks find out why Victor wanted to stage this awful scenario?"

"Mr. Sparks is to be credited with finding the how and why of that little production. Apparently, Victor was seeing this…ah, professional woman, and he paid her employers to stage that little scene. I think he planned from the beginning to make sure Megan saw it. From what Mr. Sparks told me it hadn't been difficult to arrange, since Victor was one of her regular clients."

"Oh. A prostitute." Katherine didn't try to hide the disgust in her voice. "I guess it was personal. Was it Edward or Megan he wanted to hurt?"

"Both. It seems that Victor was carrying a torch for my niece. When she married Edward, Victor began plotting to ruin him."

Shaking her head in disbelief, Katherine looked at the man she had grown to admire. It was his family that Victor Rosso had hurt. "He was in love with Megan? I wouldn't have thought him capable. He seemed so asexual. Well, I guess that fills in the blanks, all except knowing if Mr. Rosso's been permanently silenced."

Thomas placed his coffee aside, nodded. "I have made sure he will never bother any of us again. Now, young lady, let's discuss your future. I have spoken with Sandra and told her you would be leaving the company… that you have accepted my offer of a position with the Foundation." He smiled, looking directly into her eyes. He seemed to catch himself after several seconds.

"You will have to clean up your current projects, of course. And I suspect that Edward will want to take a short vacation before you two begin to establish yourselves. If I may be so bold to suggest that you see if you can take some time off as well." Nodding in agreement, Katherine wondered what exactly Sandra would heap on her before her departure.

"I will also want to establish new offices for the Foundation. As you know it has been handled by a limited staff operating out of a couple of offices located on this floor. You are going to need separate facilities, and by the time you start, the office suite will be ready. I'm refitting the office space on the file room floor. That way you will be near, but separate from Marathon Nutritionals activities. I am giving you six-week severance starting next week, and you will begin your new pay grade and benefits on the first of next month. I hope that is satisfactory!"

"Oh, wonderful. Yes, I would like to take some time off. I'll speak to Ms. Charney right away."

"Good. Then I'll look forward to having you join me tomorrow evening."

Nodding and rising, Katherine shook Thomas Sweeney's hand, holding it longer than customary. She hoped he knew just how grateful she was for everything. For her future, and graceful departure from her past. And she hoped it conveyed her desire for possibly more than just a working relationship.

Leaving the executive floor by the private elevator, no longer caring who saw her, Katherine's mind was focused on her future. She had all she could do to keep from shouting out in joy. Then reality struck, she still had to face her difficult boss.

Making a list of her open projects and preparing a status report to give Sandra Charney, she crossed her fingers hoping there would be no surprises. Next she began to address the myriad details involved in closing down Vice President Katherine Cunningham's business affairs. Sorting and cleaning out her files. Making sure any personal addresses or emails were deleted from her computer. Tossing folders containing working information on background of products and personnel she'd planned to use for future projects. She would leave all official information and documents for her successor.

Looking around her home for the past seven years, Katherine wondered what had kept her working for Sandra Charney. It had been her first step in a career she hoped would take her into a senior management position, either at Marathon or at another corporation. She'd learned a lot from her boss. Rules were good if well written, and her handling of the recent situation showed that Katherine had learned from a master. When viewed in that light, she was grateful for the experience.

33

Still somewhat high after her morning chat with Thomas, Katherine knew that the next couple of hours could still cause her grief. Settling down with an inventory of all open assignments, she was surprised to find she would be able to wrap everything up no later than Thursday. That was of course, if Ms. Charney didn't give her additional work. Now that she knew of Katherine's promotion and elevated position as Executive Vice President of the Sweeney Family Foundation, what would the Iron Maiden do? Just thinking about how Charney would react caused her stomach to clench. *Ready. Now, that first step to freedom.* Checking to make sure nothing was out in the open, she turned off her computer and with three files in hand, headed across the floor to her soon to be ex-boss's corner office.

Katherine wanted this over with and not wanting to be stalled by Alice, didn't knock before walking into Charney's outer office. "I understand that Ms. Charney is expecting me." While it wasn't true, it would require Alice to call and let Charney know that she was waiting to see her. *I just dare her to make me wait.*

"Yes, Ms. Cunningham You are expected. Go right in."

As Katherine entered the blue and white office that looked more like a showroom for modern furniture than an executive's center of power. She found Charney bent over some document and not ready to acknowledge her presence. When she finally looked up, there wasn't a hint of a wrinkle or expression on the carefully made-up face.

"Ms. Cunningham Do you have something for me?"

Katherine decided to take her cue and play it her way. "Yes, Ms. Charney." She handed her the folders. "As you can see there are three open assignments, two of which I have almost completed. I brought them with me so you could decide which of these projects you wanted me to finalize first. However, I can complete all three by the end of this week."

"I'd expect nothing less."

Shit. Was that a back-handed compliment?

"I've been looking over your schedule of projects for the balance of the quarter and find nothing that can't be taken care of by Neil." As Charney flipped through each of the folders, Katherine noticed that it had taken less than a minute before she handed them back. "As for these projects, the only one I would appreciate your completing would be the background research necessary to craft the CEOs opening statement at our annual Board of Directors meeting next month. You have researched and drafted this statement for the past six years, so it shouldn't take you too long to gather the facts and draft something for my review. Just leave the other two with Alice as you leave."

Katherine realized her boss wasn't going to mention the obvious. "I understand that Mr. Sweeney has told you that I'm leaving the company. My last day will be this Friday. However, Ms. Charney, I want you to know how much I appreciated you're taking a chance on a graduate student. I have learned many valuable lessons from you, the most important learning to thoroughly research everything prior to drafting a written paper or marketing campaign. Your training will stand me in good stead for the rest of my career."

Sandra Charney's expression hadn't changed from frozen or even hint that she appreciated Katherine's little speech of gratitude. For a moment the woman's silence seemed to echo until it reached the corners of her large office. "Ms. Cunningham, I realize I have been tougher with you than with the men in this department. You have never disappointed me. I wouldn't have promoted you to VP if I hadn't approved of your efforts to fulfill my directives."

"Thank you, Ms. Charney."

"Fine. Here is the folder for this year's statement. Complete it as you always do and leave it with Alice before you leave the company. Is there anything else?"

"No, Ms. Charney. I'll have it by Thursday at the latest."

"Then we have nothing further to discuss. I wish you luck with your work at the Foundation. Good bye."

Leaving the office in a daze, Katherine accepted that even the cool manner in which she had been dismissed hadn't been without some recognition of her past work. *Well if that was all she is capable of, it's enough.*

34

The private dining room of the Union Club was alive with smiles and good natured teasing as Thomas rose to make a toast. "Edward, now that you are retired…for health reasons…"the laughter punctuating his comment, came from those few, special people who had been invited to share in celebrating Edward Abbott's redemption and return to their clique.

"As I started to say, before causing this good humored response, was that now that Edward was no longer burdened by Marathon Nutritionals' increasingly complex financial affairs, I have asked him to accept another position. Working, with me of course. I couldn't do without Edward's counsel."

Looking at his guests Thomas announced, "Edward Abbott has agreed to become the newly established President of the Sweeney Family Foundation."

Amid the clapping and good cheer, the room waited for Thomas to continue.

"Since the Sweeney Family Foundation has just had an anonymous donation of almost $3 million…" Once again, his remarks were interrupted, as the small group began clapping amid more laughter… "We can reorganize and expand our charter. This would never have been possible without each of you and your commitment to restoring Edward's reputation. By tracking down and nailing a rat, you have protected not only Marathon, but each of us who believes in the importance of maintaining our company's first-class reputation."

The room broke out in applause.

Waiting for the table of colleagues to settle down, he continued, "I have another position at Marathon to fill, that of COO." Turning to his niece, he smiled, "OK Megan, how about taking over as Chief Operations Officer? You certainly know the job and the company."

Again the group broke out in applause. Megan looked over to her husband who was smiling broadly. "Uncle Thomas, it would be my pleasure to show you just what a woman can do." Again laughter filled the room. "Shopping isn't my thing, so I will need a challenge. I couldn't think of a more interesting use of my energy."

"Good. Now, I have one more announcement." Turning to Katherine, Thomas raised his glass once more. "Young lady, if it hadn't been for your expertise and willingness to assist Dr. Lu, John Sparks, and myself in this investigation, things could have gotten out of hand. Now that we have worked together, I believe your talents have been wasted. I am delighted that you will be Edward's right hand when he reorganizes the Foundation. I would like share your career change with our little group and let them know you have agreed to be Edward's number two at the Foundation…as his Executive Vice President."

The room broke out in round of applause as Katherine sat stunned. She hadn't expected to be singled out for her participation. She felt she had been doing her duty to the company. Now to hear that she was accepted by this group of company insiders was humbling. All she had wanted was to no longer be under Sandra Charney's thumb. That alone would have been a gift. But to work with a man she had recently gotten to know and admire, was a future she couldn't wait to begin.

"Mr. Sweeney…seeing him shake his head, she corrected herself again. "Thomas, it has been my pleasure to help Edward put this unfortunate situation behind him. To work with him will truly be my pleasure."

Everyone in the room stood. "To Katherine," they sang in unison.

Thomas raised his glass again. "A toast. To new beginnings. New friends, and better times ahead." He said, looking directly at Katherine.

As she looked around the table and watched Shen Lu, John Sparks, Edward and Megan join in drinking to his toast, Katherine felt she had been accepted into a family. One, not of blood, but born of friendship.

THE END

Acknowledgements

The creation of *TBD* –*to be determined*- was made possible by the encouragement and guidance of Maya Sloan award winning author and instructor of advanced novel writing. Under her guidance I was able to nurture a kernel of an idea into a fully realized novel.

Writing is a solitary endeavor and as such I am fortunate to have a small but close group of friends who provided ongoing comments and suggestions during the entire writing process. They are Susan Wayne, Linda Paternoster, Joy Smith and Elinor Ruskin...each prolific readers and experienced in the world of public relations and corporate communications. In addition, Mary Karpin author and friend, helped to polish some of the twists and turns of the escalating drama. Leona Kelly who alerted me to some of the changes in off-shore banking regulations being made by the IRS, and her non-corporate reader's suggestions in depicting some of the business aspects of the story.

My thanks and gratitude to Mr. Bruce Hulme, private investigator, retired, for providing me with an overview of how my fictional PI might approach his search to uncover the blackmailer, and for helping me to accurately plot his steps in following leads that one-by-one led to his downfall.

I would also like to thank Kathy Rygg, author, skilled editor and longtime friend for her continuing support in the midst of her own active life.

As an author I use words to paint pictures so it is especially gratifying to have accomplished designer and illustrator, Jesse Horowitz create a cover to crystalize my tale of corporate intrigue.

www.ingramcontent.com/pod-product-compliance
Lightning Source LLC
Chambersburg PA
CBHW071553110726
47908CB00007B/2086